CROSS CUT

PRAISE FOR WES RAND

"The unconventional collected works of Wes Rand was recommended to me. I can say these are not for the whimsical as you'll wish that only bandits, outlaws, and wildlife, are the only things to fear. Bring a gun as you sit down to read and pray you are not on the wrong side of Major Neville Stryker."

— **DIANE KAWASAKI**, WRITER AND STAR OF
TLC'S HIT SHOW MY LITTLE LIFE

"Gritty, dark, and fast-paced—If you love frontier action, Wes Rand's EVIL STRYKER SERIES will knock you out of the saddle."

— *ERIC J. GUIGNARD*, AWARD-WINNING
AUTHOR, AND EDITOR, INCLUDING *AFTER
DEATH...* AND *BAGGAGE OF ETERNAL NIGHT*,
BRAM STOKER AWARD-WINNER

"As a filmmaker, I can see the vibrant images come to life on every page as Evil Stryker crosses every line of decency and yet leaves the women wanting him and the men wanting to be him. Wes has created an anti-hero of devastating impact."

— **VINCENT ROCCA**, WRITER/DIRECTOR OF
KISSES AND CAROMS, AUTHOR OF *11 SIMPLE
STEPS TO TURN A SCREENPLAY INTO A
MARKETABLE MOVIE: OR, HOW I GOT A $10K
MOVIE TO GROSS $1 MILLION THROUGH WARNER
BROS*

ALSO BY WES RAND

CROSS CUT

Book II in the Evil Stryker Series

WES RAND

CROSS CUT -

BOOK 2 IN THE EVIL STRYKER SERIES

Second Edition

Copyright © 2021 by Wes Rand

Cover Copyright © 2021 by Wes Rand

All Rights Reserved.

Cover Illustration and Design by Konstantin Yastrebov

Editing Services and Formatting: Stacey Smekofske EditsByStacey.com

Paperback ISBN: 978-1-7362400-4-5

Digital ISBN: 978-1-7362400-5-2

Published by Wild West Books

Printed in the United States of America.

To All Military Veterans.

CHAPTER ONE

The Heritage Trail ran between Tahoe and Roseville, curved away from a wooded ridge, and wound its way toward lower elevations. The lone rider saw Auburn's lights about a mile ahead. Ever watchful, he let the big roan horse pick its way down the sloped trail. Eventually, the trail left the trees and entered a wide valley with rolling, grassy hills. He reined in and studied the landscape ahead, where steel rails wound through the hills and telegraph poles stretched out a line of crosses along the tracks. The trail converged with a service road beside the rails. Stryker abandoned the trail, cut across open ground, and followed the road west toward Auburn. The lean, six foot-three-inch man rode easily in a weathered saddle, slick and shiny from hard use. The leather skirt hanging beneath it once held the stamped-on name of MAJOR NEVILLE STRYKER. But letters had weathered away over the years. What remained was a better fit for the man he'd become—EVIL STRYKER.

His black shirt and denim pants looked worn and used, like the .44 Colt Peacemaker held snug to his right hip. A straight razor in his back pocket was used for shaving, mostly. A .44-40 Winchester hung in the rifle boot, but a sinister fork-like weapon, carried in the small of his back, had been particularly useful against sword during the Civil War and spear in the Indian campaigns. He'd learned fighting skills from his uncle, an Asian master in the ancient martial arts form of Kung Fu. The sai had a twelve-inch center tine and two shorter ones on each side, all filed to needle point sharpness. Normally, two sai were used. Stryker carried a single sai, two being impractical in the pouch behind his back. More than one man, when drawing his last breath, had marveled at the blood-soaked prongs.

The sharp-boned face, weathered like the saddle with lines etched by years in the western sun, was framed by a week-old beard. His mustache drooped at the corners, Mexican style. Black hair hung straight, brushing his shoulders from under a low-brimmed Stetson, also black, but sweat stained and dust covered. Staring out between prominent cheekbones and sharp ridges of his brows, his pale gray eyes were as intense as an eagle's.

He'd unfurled his bedroll in another evening of an unrelenting week-long drizzle. What rations he had left, salt pork and soggy biscuits, were nearly gone, and he'd boiled coffee using the same grounds for five days. The rain had stopped three hours earlier, but the thought of a hot meal and dry warm bed was too tempting for him to spend another night in camp. He calculated two more days to Sacramento, then perhaps five days more to reach San Francisco.

Although, at the age of seven, he had witnessed Woolen Mill workers butcher his parents near Fisherman's Wharf, San Francisco remained the closest thing to his having a home. His mother's brother had taken over his upbringing, schooling young Neville outside the classroom with useful fighting skills, but the uncle had long since died as well. Almost twenty-five years had passed and none of his European father's or his Asian-Mexican mother's kin remained alive in California. Still, in his mind, it was home.

Even though his stay in the last town, Egalitaria, lasted only a few days, what happened there drove him further away from the man he'd once been. He tried not to dwell on the past—his having been a happily married ex-military officer with a promising career at J.P. Morgan's bank. "All over," he'd said to himself. Leigh, and several of his wife's family had been killed, some fault of his, but their deaths due mostly to acts of another man . . . a man he subsequently killed. A sardonic smile briefly cracked Stryker's lips, and he released a wad of spit. Since then, he'd become a wanted man, always on the run. *Worth it.* But, brutally tragic events plagued his life, relentless, transforming him into something akin to a wounded animal, vicious and short-tempered. He also became an efficient killer. Few foes got a second chance.

The sun set about an hour before he entered town. Auburn was a boom town during the forty-niner gold rush and still ran rail service. Trains traveled east and west between Promontory Point and Sacramento. Although Auburn had declined since its boom days, it still sported two saloons, as well as a bank, a jail, and a dry goods store. Other than the blacksmith in back of the dry goods, the rest of the businesses and shops had closed when the gold ran out. Stryker dismounted at a water trough and let the roan suck water. After the horse drank, he attached a halter rope and led the animal down the street. He passed up a single-story watering hole and pulled up in front of the two-story Rich Bitch Saloon.

Gloria, who owned the place, wasn't rich nowadays, but she kept the name tacked on the building. The sound of piano music and raucous banter of card play drifted out from behind the closed doors. Four horses and one mule stood out front. Stryker looped the rope over a rail, scraped his boots, and climbed three pine planks to the Rich Bitch. He pushed open the door and surveyed the room. The smell of stale beer and tobacco smoke that lingered in wide drifting ribbons rushed to greet him. A well-stoked fire glowed in a pot-bellied stove by the left wall. A long ornate bar stretched along the opposite wall.

The piano fell silent along with the saloon occupants who turned their attention to the man who'd just entered. Stryker eyed each occupant, then headed for the bar.

He walked past a table with a man drinking by himself and another table where four men played cards. Five of the eight remaining tables were also occupied with drinking card players.

Saloon girls, perched on the laps of groping men, solicited drinks. The men probably knew the drinks were overpriced but figured grabbing handfuls of tits and ass worth the extra money.

When Stryker stopped at the counter, the men returned to their drinking, gambling, and groping. A man drinking alone, solidly built in his late forties, continued to watch Stryker. He wore a black overcoat with a forest-green velvet collar, unbuttoned and spread open to reveal a brown corduroy waistcoat and matching trousers. Sipping a tall mug of beer, his eyes followed the mixed-breed across the room. He glanced nervously at the other men before returning his attention to the tall stranger.

Two dance hall girls, a redhead and a short-haired blonde whose hair badly needed a wash, sat on the stairs leading to the second floor. Leaning forward, they rested their elbows on knees spread apart and smoked cheroots. Both appeared past their prime, but Gloria let them stay on, providing they earned enough to pay for room and board, and smokes.

The redhead nudged the blonde and nodded toward Stryker. "He's all yours, honey."

"He looks kinda rough, Ruthie." The blonde scrunched up her face, took a long drag on the cheroot, and exhaled with resignation. "Ah, what the hell." She threw the butt in a beer glass and pushed herself upright.

Stryker glimpsed the stairs as he took off his coat. He raised a boot onto the brass rail and leaned against the countertop. The bartender, a corpulent man who looked to be in his early fifties said, "Yeah, mister?"

"Whiskey."

The bartender grabbed a shot glass from underneath the counter and slapped it on top of the bar.

Across the room, the blonde descended the stairs and sauntered over to stand by Stryker. Resting an arm on his shoulder, she asked, "You gonna drink all by yourself?"

Stryker glanced at her and then turned to watch the bartender fill his glass.

"Pretty lonely on the trail, ain't it?" Getting no response, she said, "I'm Leda." She traced circles around the back of Stryker's shoulder with her fingers. "Me, I don't like to drink alone. How about buying me something and we can talk for a while?" She gave the ends of his black hair a little jerk.

The saloonkeeper filled Stryker's shot glass, draining what was left in the bottle, and set up another. He left the empty on the counter, and then brought out a second one labeled whiskey, but it held tea. He filled Leda's glass with the tea and slid it toward her.

Before Stryker could push through cheap toilet water and cheroot breath to give a reply, a man coming down the stairs, called out to her, "Leda, we ain't done yet!"

A freckled-faced man in his early twenties fumbled with his shirt buttons as he bounded barefooted down the stairs. A sheriff's badge hung cockeyed on the white shirt. A handsome fellow and wearing nattily clothes, Stryker figured the badge was more show than law enforcement. The young sheriff hitched up his trousers with his gun belt thrown over his shoulder. Stryker remained watchful, tracking the man's movement from the corner of his eye.

Ruthie jumped up and grabbed his arm. "Troy, no!" She hung on, her feet taking staccato steps down the stairs. Troy reached the bottom step with his shirt half buttoned.

"Leda!"

"You fell asleep, Troy!" Leda pressed against Stryker.

"That don't mean I'm quittin." Troy shook Ruthie off his arm and stomped across the floor toward Leda and Stryker. He came in a straight line, knocking tables and chairs out of his way.

The card players erupted in guffaws and one yelled, "Hey, Troy, you pass out from too much blood in your pecker? Or did it go to sleep too?" The men roared louder.

Troy ignored the jeers and reached for Leda's arm, but she jerked away and wedged herself between Stryker and the bar.

"Let go of her, mister. Me and her got unfinished business." Troy grabbed Stryker's shoulder and yanked.

The mixed-breed reached for the glass but drew his arm back and jammed an elbow into Leda's ribcage.

"Whoaaa!" The air gushed from Leda's lungs, and she staggered several steps along the bar before she could catch her breath. Finally, she managed to inhale and cough.

"Oh my God!" Leda gasped, holding a hand flat against her breastbone and gripping the edge of the bar with the other to keep from falling.

"You bastard!" Troy let go of Stryker's shoulder, drew back his fist.

Stryker snatched the empty whiskey bottle and shattered it against Troy's forehead. Glass and the remnants of stale whiskey exploded on the sheriff's face. Stryker lunged with the broken bottle.

Troy recoiled, and the jagged edge sliced an ear. Stryker twisted the broken glass, slashing the man's jaw, and the sharp tip counted teeth as it ripped out his mouth.

A flap of cheek spilled open. Troy slapped the side of his face, shocked to feel his teeth through the gaping wound.

"Shit! You cut . . ." The words bubbled out in a torrent of blood. Troy's bloodied hand grabbed for the revolver hanging over his shoulder.

Stryker dropped the broken bottle and in a single move, drew, cocked, and fired. The .44 slug tore into Troy's chest before the glass shard clinked against the brass rail. The blast knocked Troy backward. He gathered his balance, staggered a step toward Stryker, pitched forward, and collapsed on the beer-soaked floor.

"Troy!" Leda shrieked. "Oh, no, Troy!" Sobbing, she flung herself on his back, burying her face between his shoulders, and wrapping her arms around the dying man. She lifted her tear-stained face and screamed at Stryker, "You killed him, you bastard!" She fell on Troy again and called out his name over and over until Stryker sent a boot crashing against her temple.

Stryker thumbed the hammer of the Colt and raked the barrel around the saloon. He hesitated, waiting for the distinct click of another gun's action. Hearing none, he gathered up his coat and stepped sideways toward the front door.

After Stryker left the saloon, a single patron rose and followed him out, closing the door behind him. He let the mixed-breed mount the roan before he spoke.

"You want employ?"

Stryker recognized him as the man who sat alone in the saloon. He'd earlier noted the man was unarmed. Still, he faced the man as he pulled on his coat. He booted the stirrup, hoisted himself into the saddle, and then leaned forward, resting his forearms on the saddle horn. He kept a watchful eye on the door; however, the ruckus coming from those inside suggested their most immediate concern was the dead man and the unconscious woman.

"I just wore out my welcome," Stryker grunted.

"You could be right. Not staying in town too. Besides, *das* law is on *der* floor in *der* saloon with a hole in him. I travel to Santa Cruz County and need protection."

"All right, German man, expecting a train robbery." Stryker often asked questions with statements.

"Not taking train, not from here *any-vay*. Name's Hans Hihn." Hihn spoke with a German accent, jerky and clipped. Although middle-aged, his five feet-ten-inch body appeared solid and in shape. He had an angular face and a receding hairline. "I have three wagons about three miles from town. I meet my brother in Sacramento, secure a Dolbeer steam donkey to haul to San Jose, then to Felton."

"Felton." Stryker repeated, and then added, "Steam donkey."

"North of Santa Cruz, *die* town. It is south of Big Basin and *die* tall trees. Three days to Sacramento, two to get supplies, could be sixteen to Felton. Three weeks or a day or two more." Hihn, noting that Stryker still waited in the saddle, described the machine. "Steam donkey is steam operated engine used to haul logs."

"Pay."

"Ten dollars for day, *vith* meals, and lodging."

"Forty dollars a day, a third now."

"Good Christ Almighty!"

"Take it or leave it." Stryker said, sitting up and pulling on the reins.

"Wait a minute now. Uh . . . we better leave. Let me get my mule. I *vill* pay your price mister . . .?"

"Stryker."

"If I get killed, you *vill* not be paid." Hihn warned.

"Give me something to shoot for."

Hihn brought the mule alongside the boardwalk and looped the halter rope over its long ears. He grabbed a fistful of coarse mane and swung himself onto the bare back. Goading the mule into the middle of the street, he looked back and said, "Mister Stryker, you probably don't know that steam donkey is both' loved and hated in *das* log business. But cannot be hated more than this damn mule. I tell you more in camp, if mule does not shake out my teeth out my head."

Hihn bounced down the street on the trotting mule, heading west out of town. He didn't look back to see if Stryker followed.

CHAPTER TWO

Stryker didn't push the roan. The moon shone brightly on a cloudless night, and he easily kept Hihn in sight. However, if he lost sight of him, he could probably still hear the German cursing the mule. He kept at least two lengths behind him. Missing out on a hot bath and a warm bed in Auburn soured him, and he was in no mood for talk.

There had been a few brief moments in Egalitaria, when he glimpsed a better life. He'd been hired on and promised a considerable sum of money by a fine-looking woman. Once again, fate intervened; both the money and the woman were gone.

The last time he'd had a bath and a bed to sleep on was in Egalitaria, and Morgan Bickford had shared it. He couldn't help thinking about how she moved under him. She'd cut a business deal. She also used her body to get what she wanted. He liked that about her. A corner of his mouth twitched.

Stryker was to receive forty percent of the proceeds from selling her mine and ranch. Money he never collected. But his concern meant more than the money. He had to admit it. The loss of Morgan bore an even deeper hole in him. No one had affected him like that since Leigh, his deceased wife of some fifteen years. Memories of Leigh haunted him, but Morgan changed things. Now she was dead too, like Leigh, a collateral casualty.

He wouldn't make that mistake again.

Hihn stopped the mule and slid to the ground. The three miles passed quickly. Lost in thought, Stryker hadn't realized how far they'd traveled until Hihn started across an open field, leading the mule. Stryker dismounted from the roan, pulled the .44-.40, and followed.

The full moon allowed Stryker to see deep wagon ruts scarring the level ground, and it appeared more than one heavy wagon had made them. He and Hihn rounded a small hill and three wagons came into view, a Conestoga and two freight wagons. Tethered along a rope line that stretched out behind the wagons, the mules snorted greetings.

"Tend to your horse. I *vill* tie der mule and built *der* fire. You hungry?" Hihn asked as he secured the mule on the rope line.

"Sure."

"Hasenpfeffer soup. Skinny rabbit," Hihn warned.

Hihn rebuilt the fire and heated coffee next to the stew pot. Stryker joined him, throwing his saddle down not far from the fire.

Hihn filled his own bowl and cup and pointed at a camp table holding dishes and utensils.

Stryker ladled the aromatic stew into a wooden bowl and poured himself a steaming cup of coffee. He sat and stretched out his legs, and after crossing them, he leaned back against his saddle to eat. When he'd washed down the last spoonful of stew with the coffee he said, "Rabbit died for a good cause." He placed the bowl beside him on the ground. "What's in the wagons?"

"Rigging for *der* steam donkey, supplies, feed for *die* mules."

Stryker got to his feet, still holding the cup. He threw the remaining coffee down his throat and said, "Must be a heavy load. Tell me about the steam donkey." He lifted the pot from the grate, refilled his cup, and headed for the Conestoga.

"Used to pull logs out to *der* . . . Hey! Hold on, Mister! I told you what is in it!"

But Stryker was already standing behind the wagon, looking in.

"If you come in, I'll shoot," a female voice warned from the darkened interior. Stryker couldn't clearly see the woman with only a feint German accent. He could see the shotgun, though. He leaned against the tailgate, sipping from the cup.

She continued, "I know it may not be the first time you've had a gun pointed at you, but it'll be the last time if you . . ."

"Curious about the heavy load. How wide's your ass?" Stryker cut in.

A second female giggled.

"Shut up, Kahla," said the first.

"My name's Kahla. The one who's going to shoot you is Rachel. Her ass is bigger than mine." The accent was the same as Rachel's.

"Shut up, Kahla."

"Any more . . ." Stryker began.

"My daughters, Rachel and Kahla," Hihn interrupted, coming around to peer into the wagon. "I intend to perform introductions in *der* morning. Girls, this is Mister Stryker. He *vill* ride with us. Rachel, you can put the shotgun away." Looking at Stryker, he said. "You meet them in der morning." Hihn swiveled his head toward the wagon's interior, keeping his eyes on Stryker. "Go back to sleep, girls. Come with me, Stryker." The German started back to the campfire.

Stryker pushed away from the tailgate.

"I sleep under one of *die* wagons," Hihn said, poking the fire with a stick. "Stryker, you probably *vonder* why I hire you instead of *der* other men in *der* saloon. Why *vould* I trust you, since you meet my daughters? They are not my daughters. They are my nieces. After *die* mother and father died of diphtheria, I bring them to America and raise 'em. My wife died six years ago. Now it is just us three. Way you treat that woman in *der* saloon told me you had something bother you inside and it do not appear you look for female companionship. That is good, got enough trouble."

"I'll move my horse and gear out a ways, toward the trail. Be coming in for at sunup," Stryker said.

"We *vill* have *der* coffee ready," Hihn acted relieved that Stryker stood guard between the wagons and the road — and not near his nieces.

Stryker slung his saddle onto the roan and girded it, but led the horse on foot to a large clump of boulders near the road. There, he tethered the roan to a scrub oak surrounded by tall wet grass. He pulled the saddle and carried it a few feet away before throwing it on the ground and unfurling his bedroll. After sliding the Peacemaker and the Winchester beside him under the blanket, he closed his eyes and tried to sleep. He never slept well.

It'd been years. Leigh's bloodied face, her shattered body–the images were branded in his head. He'd found his wife as the last moments of life drained away. She died with his name on her lips.

Even killing the man, who'd primarily caused her death, couldn't cut the grief.

Morning arrived with low hanging fog blanketing the area. The recent rain left heavy dew, soaking the ground and vegetation, and leaving Stryker's bedroll and gear damp. He'd slept on the saddle blanket. At least it was dry. He placed it onto the roan's back and threw on the saddle. Stryker smelled the wood smoke from the campfire before he saw its bluish column curling above the treetops. And whatever was being cooked for breakfast permeated the brisk morning air with a tempting aroma. As he led the roan closer to camp, he could hear Hihn cursing the mules. When he got within sight of the wagons, he stopped, surveyed the surroundings, and then walked on into camp. He paused briefly to watch the German work the mules.

Hihn led a pair of mules over and positioned them in front of the Conestoga. "Back." Hihn held the lead halter on one of the mules and pulled down and back. "Back, you stubborn animal." He pushed its muscular chest with his hand. "Back!" After harnessing the collar, he hitched the mule to the wagon. He harnessed and hitched the rest of the mules, four to the Conestoga, and a team of eight to the conjoined freight wagons. It took more time and a lot more cursing.

Stryker tethered the roan opposite the wagons, grabbed a cup from his saddlebag, carrying it to the cooking fire. He'd just reached for the coffeepot when one of the girls stepped out of the Conestoga carrying a covered pan. He filled his cup and set the pot back on the grate. After sipping the coffee, Stryker lowered the cup and waited, watching her walk toward him.

"Good morning, Mister Stryker." She said cheerfully. "Those are runzas in the skillet, dough pockets filled with cabbage and meat. The meat is grisly hardtack, but the cabbage is still green. Drink your coffee while they cook. Be a few more minutes."

"You're Rachel."

"Does my backside look that big?" She scowled playfully, offering a saucy pout.

"Recognized your voice. Haven't seen your ass." He thought Rachel looked to be in her early twenties with hair so blonde it seemed white in the early morning light. Face a little too round, high cheekbones, blue eyes, and a stout frame that would probably carry more weight in her middle age.

Rachel studied him a moment before replying. Seeing his hard features in daylight may have caused her to hesitate. "You're going all the way to Felton?"

"Maybe."

"A dirty, smelly little sawmill town named after a politician. Shoulda' been called Sawmill, no . . . Dog Poop Junction! That's what it smells like." Stryker figured the female voice inside the wagon to be Kahla's.

"Kahla didn't much care for it. Can't say I do either. It stinks." Rachel shoveled a runza onto a tin plate and handed it to Stryker. "See if you like these."

Stryker set his coffee on a flat rock by his feet and took the plate. He lifted the dough pocket from the tin and tried a small bite for heat and taste, then finished the runza in three big mouthfuls. Rachel watched patiently, her raised eyebrows asking for approval. She got a nod. Stryker leaned down, laid the plate on the rock, grabbed his coffee, and walked away.

Rachel poured a cup of coffee, dished another runza onto a plate, and brought both over to Hihn. He stopped cursing at the mules and wiped his hands on his pants before taking the food.

"Thank you, fräulein. Took longer this morning. Mules acting strange. You girls ready?"

"Yes, why don't you get him to help?" Rachel asked, looking at Stryker.

"I do not think he knows about mules, but if he does, he *vould* not help." Hihn paused, bit into the runza, and tracked Rachel's line of sight toward the mixed-breed. I saw him kill a man last night. I hired him for his gun. I feel he thinks the same. Do not annoy him."

Rachel studied Stryker for several long minutes before starting the clean-up. "Kahla, there's one left. If you want it, you better get out here."

"Coming." Kahla jumped out the back of the wagon and ran to the cook fire.

Stryker didn't bother turning to see the younger fräulein. If he had, he would have seen a woman thinner in face and body, prettier, and more slender than her older sister. Kahla had the same blonde hair, and her face seemed to always display impish humor.

"Is it hot?" Kahla asked, bending down and warming her hands by the fire.

"Should be." Rachel glanced at Stryker, whose back was turned to her while he inspected the roan. "Kahla, that man has the eyes of a ghost."

Kahla grabbed the last runza from the pan and bit into it. "He looks like a man to me."

Stryker gulped down the last of his coffee and strolled over to the fire. He glanced at the sisters as he put his cup next to the empty runza pan. "Obliged."

The girls stood opposite the fire pit, offering friendly smiles, perhaps expecting more conversation, but Stryker abruptly left to go talk with Hihn.

"I'll be about a half mile ahead. If I need you to get off the trail, I'll either come back to tell you or fire two quick shots. If you hear the shots, pull off and stay put until I return." Stryker said to Hihn.

"Me and my fräuleins *vill* be on the road in half hour. They *vill* lead with *der* Conestoga and I *vill* bring on *der* freight wagons. I know I should travel in front, but they complain about *der* dust. It *vill* be hard to hear any shots over racket mules and wagons make, but I *vill* tell the girls to listen for them. We *vill* need to water *die* animals about midday."

"Tell Rachel to keep a shotgun close. What do you have, Hihn?"

"A rifle and a pistol. I don't think those troublemakers *vill* be this far out. Better watch out for bandits."

"Bandits?" Stryker asked.

"Banditos, mostly Mexicans. Used to be very bad, thirty-five, maybe forty years ago, 'til they got run out of San Francisco. Hanged several, and they fled like rats to Los Angeles. Two thousand of them go south. There is still few up here. All is left is young ones. Rode *der* train out but did not see them. Der real trouble *vill* be in Felton, Stryker."

CHAPTER THREE

The roan pranced skittishly with Stryker hopping alongside beside it with one boot in the stirrup. Rachel and Kahla, their arms loaded with pots and pans, stopped and watched. They burst out laughing. "Hey Stryker!" Kahla hooted. "You gonna ride that horse or just dance with him?" Hihn, busy with the mules, didn't watch the horse-and-man two-step.

Stryker began to suspect something spooked the horse. The mules had given Hihn trouble, too. He pulled his foot from the stirrup and led the roan past Hihn. "Animals smelling something." He walked back out to the trail and booted the stirrup again. However, the animal still acted skittish after Stryker managed to scramble into the saddle. The roan made two tight circles before Stryker dug his heels in its flanks and then it bolted onto the trail, heading west.

A mile later the roan slowed to a canter, its muzzle foaming, its sides heaving and lathered. Stryker reined it to a walk. He scanned the trail ahead from right to left, left to right, one hundred and eighty degrees, drawing concentric arcs with his eyes. When he had satisfied himself, there was no immediate threat ahead. He pulled the roan around and faced it rearward. He couldn't yet see Hihn or the wagons on the trail.

While Stryker sat in the saddle resting the roan, he breathed deeply, taking in the crisp aroma of Ponderosa and Douglas. Other trees like Big Leaf Maples and Canyon Oaks had yet to sprout buds on their branches, but signs of an early spring were clear. He headed the roan uphill to the sound of rushing water, the big horse bobbing its head with each step. The creek spilled down the slope through heavy deer brush before turning parallel to the trail a half mile down. Stryker figured the higher elevation would afford him better viewing over the stand of short trees cloistered two hundred yards to his front.

He gained two hundred feet in altitude, found flat ground under a Maple tree, dismounted, and swapped bit and bridle with a halter from his saddlebag before tethering the horse to a low branch. The animal would have to cool down first, and then it could be watered. In the meantime, he'd wipe it down and keep an eye out for trouble from higher ground.

After pulling the saddle and sweat drenched blanket, Stryker retrieved the burlap sack Rachel had placed by his saddlebags that morning. He put the contents, hardtack wrapped in waxed paper, a few whole potatoes, and three cans of beans, on a rock out of reach from the roan. The stream was a couple hundred feet away, and he headed toward it as he scanned the landscape and road. He soaked the sack in the cold water and walked back. Stryker made several more trips before he got the animal washed down. He made one more trip to rinse the sackcloth and then brought the horse to water. A good part of an hour had passed since he had left the wagons. They ought to come into sight soon, he figured. He loaded the grub into his saddlebag, hung the sack outside to dry, and re-saddled the roan.

Stryker put a boot in the stirrup when suddenly the horse reared. He tried to push himself clear, but the twisted stirrup trapped his boot. The big horse went high, pulling Stryker's wedged foot to his shoulder and jerking him off the ground. He swung under the roan's belly, his head and shoulders striking hard against the rocky soil. When the hooves came down, narrowly missing him, he clawed at the strapping, struggling to plant his free foot. The roan broke away at a full gallop, dragging him with his leg locked in the stirrup. Stryker got a hand on his boot top, but a hoof grazed his temple and everything turned black. His body bounced along the ground until he smashed into a hard mound of dirt. That ripped the boot free.

Then the grizzly was on him.

Stryker lay face down and it leapt onto his shoulders. The beast raked its teeth across the back of his head, crunching bone as it slashed open his scalp. Four-inch claws laid open his ribs through three layers of clothing. Moving down the body, the animal bit into the buttocks and lifted Stryker from the ground. It shook his limp body twice and let go. One last bite into a calf and the bear loped up the hill, back to her two cubs.

⤬

"That looks like Mister Stryker's horse." Kahla yelled to her sister.

Rachel had been staring at the lead mules' ears and the road ahead between them. "Whoa." She yanked hard on the traces and booted the wagon brake. The wagon clamor tailed off to isolated harness rattling and animal snorting.

Kahla pointed, "See? Over there."

Rachel first looked at Kahla, and then she saw the roan. "It *is* his horse. Something's happened."

Hihn brought his wagon alongside, "Why did you stop?"

"That's Mister Stryker's horse."

The roan turned toward them upon reaching the road and Rachel, still holding the traces, nodded towards the big horse.

"Pull your *vagon* over to those trees. I *vill* swing mine around and come up behind you." Hihn briefly scanned the landscape ahead before goading the mules with a snap of the traces. "Yaa. Gee." A worried look came over his face as he swung his mules toward the stand of aspens.

By the time they reached the trees and Hihn roped his mules to the girls' wagon, the roan had turned onto the road two hundred feet away and was coming on at a hard gallop. Hihn ran to the road, waving his arms to cut off the fleeing horse.

"*Vhoa! Vhoa* there!"

It didn't stop, but it swerved and slowed down, coming to a stop about two hundred feet up a grassy rise. Hihn scrambled up to it. He grabbed the reins and lead the frightened animal over to the wagons.

"Something frightened him!" Hihn yelled as he hitched the roan to the rear of the freight wagon. "I'm leaving *der* horse here, cannot ride him. Gimme *der* shotgun."

Kahla reached behind the seat, grabbed the Greener twelve-gauge and handed it to Rachel, who passed it on to Hihn.

"You girls stay in *der* wagon. Did you see where he came from?"

Kahla pointed and said, "The trees on that far hill? Looks like he ran out from them."

"Be careful, Hihny." Kahla added.

"Get *das* rifle from my wagon." Then Hihn changed his mind. "Hold on, I *vill* get it." Hihn retrieved the Winchester and handed it to Rachel. "It is loaded. Use it if you have to. I *vill* not be long."

Hihn carried the weapon at the ready and set off for the trees. He crossed a gully and climbed up the other side, coming up to a small escarpment of boulders, and he spotted the stream flowing out from aspens and pine trees.

"Stryker!" Hihn crouched behind the rocks. "Stryker!"

Hihn waited a couple more minutes, listening for a response. No answer. He eased out from behind the boulders and crept forward. He was almost to the trees up on the hill when he saw the prone figure on the ground not more than forty feet away. He crouched low and ran toward Stryker. When he reached him, he realized no one had shot him, but the dark pool around Stryker indicated serious blood loss. His first thought was that Stryker had been scalped, but the top of his head was still intact. However, the back was laid open showing white bone. Ragged gashes across his bloodied coat indicated an animal attack. Then Hihn discovered the grizzly's tracks nearby.

Kahla saw Hihn coming down the hill first. He came walking fast, jumping over the low brush, casting quick glances over his shoulder. "He's coming back!"

"Grizzly!" Hihn shouted when he got within range. "Grizzly got him."

"He's dead?" Rachel asked.

"Looked it. He *vill* be if he not already." Hihn didn't stop at the girl's wagon. He untied the mules, climbed into the freight wagon, and brought it even with the other wagon.

"You sure?" Kahla's voice rose.

"We cannot do nothing for him. That bear tore him bad and might come back. Go."

Hihn goaded his mules forward. "Yaa!" He swung the team into the lead and headed for the road. Upon reaching it, Hihn turned right. "Gee."

He'd gone a half mile and then looked behind to check on his nieces.

"Ah, damn."

The girls weren't on the trail. He spotted their wagon crawling up the hill toward Stryker.

By the time Hihn rode back and started up the hill following the girls' wagon, his nieces had reached Stryker. Up ahead, Kahla crouched with the Winchester pointed up the hill. She stood guard while Rachel knelt by the wounded man.

"Hihny's right. He's pretty bad," Rachel said as she placed her fingers on Stryker's neck. "But he's alive."

Rachel and Kahla steeled themselves for the gruesome scene they were sure to find, but if they were to disobey their uncle, they couldn't let him find them showing weakness. Flies had begun to buzz around the wounds and the stench of congealed blood mixed with lingering bear's odor churned the stomach.

"I feel like I'm gonna throw up," Kahla said, letting go of the rifle barrel and covered her mouth with her hand. The Winchester drooped downward, and she gripped its front again, pressing her mouth and nose against the inside of her elbow. "It smells awful." Kahla moaned, her speech muffled by her coat sleeve.

"Let's get him in the wagon before we clean him up." Rachel said, standing up. She peered into the trees with an anxious scowl.

"How?" Kahla asked.

"You girls get his legs and I *vill* get his shoulders." Hihn said, coming up behind.

Kahla spun around. "You came back!" she said, sounding surprised and relieved.

"First, let us roll him over. Each of you grab him by the knees," Hihn instructed. He continued talking as the three lifted Stryker off the ground. "When we get him in *der* wagon, Kahla, you drive. Rachel, see what you can do to clean him. I have a bottle of whisky in my box. Use it to clean the wounds. A doctor in Philadelphia said that *vould* stop infection. If he wakes up, pour some in him. And save me a swallow. Do not waste it all on a dead man."

They carried Stryker to the Conestoga. Kahla and Rachel eased his legs to the ground and dropped the tailgate. Then the three of them maneuvered the two-hundred-pound man onto the floorboard. Hihn clasped his hands together to boost Rachel into the wagon and then raised the tailgate. Hihn hurriedly shuffled back to the freight wagons and Kahla ran to the front of the Conestoga.

Hihn motioned for Kahla to lead off down the hill. He followed her wagon to the road and continued to let her lead. He figured the grizzly was long gone, but the real reason he put the girls in front was to keep dust down in their wagon.

Rachel climbed in beside Stryker and arranged a makeshift bed. She removed what was left of his coat and shirts before turning Stryker over on his stomach. She washed out the scalp and rib wounds with the whisky before noticing the rips in the pant seat and leg. Upon working his trousers off she discovered the leg bites weren't as deep as first appeared, but she used the whisky on them as well, swabbing out the puncture wounds as best she could.

Kahla glanced backward when the mules were on a straight, smoother stretch of road and saw Stryker lying face down. "Damn."

"Yeah, they're bad. I washed them out, but who knows? His head's the worst. I had to put the scalp pieces back in place." Rachel said, applying a dressing to Stryker's head.

Kahla returned her attention to the mules. "I wasn't talking about the cuts," she said to herself.

"I cleaned him up with the whiskey and got rid of the bear's odor. Now he just smells like a drunk," Rachel said, plopping down beside Kahla. "He needs a doctor. He's lost a lot of blood."

"Hihny says three days to Sacramento," Kahla said.

"We'll put him in the ground before we get there," Rachel said.

CHAPTER FOUR

Three times during the day, Kahla tried to give Stryker water. However, her efforts were mostly limited to moistening his lips with a wet cloth. The women kept their words to a minimum, content to watch the trail and mull over events in silence. Other than checking on Stryker every few hours, neither mentioned the injured man. The younger woman saw Stryker as a new adventure, the older one, a curiosity.

Hihn halted the wagons, once to rest and water the mules, and again for the night with two hours of daylight left. The interruption that morning made for a shortened travel day. He figured they faced two and a half more days' travel before reaching Sacramento. By the time Hihn unhitched the mules and got them fed and watered, the sun sank beneath the forested hills. Rachel built a fire ring out of small stones and placed a coffee pot on the Swedish torch log. Hihn normally built more traditional fires, but Rachel found a suitable log and she used it, saving time and effort.

"He's still breathing." Kahla said, approaching the fire.

"If he's gonna live, it'll be up to him. Not much else we can do." Rachel said, while stirring meat and potatoes in the skillet. "I changed the bandages. Used more whiskey, and he didn't flinch when I poured it in the cuts."

"Damn," Kahla said.

"Save me some, *vill* you?" Hihn ordered, positioning a rock for a seat. "Get plenty sleep. We'll start out earlier in *der* morning than today. How you girls gonna do *die* sleeping arrangements? I'm not unloading *der* wagon. One of you can sleep *vith* me under on the ground."

"That'll be you, Kahla," Rachel said.

"Why me?" Kahla's voice rose. "Why can't Rachel?"

"For goodness sake. Take turns. If *der* man lives, you can switch tomorrow night. Some bodyguard he is now," Hihn groused.

Tension built during the meal. Even though Stryker had only spent one night with them, he had provided a sense of security they had not known before he arrived. Now, without him, their vulnerability became more noticeable. Hihn wore an angry scowl and groused continuously about Stryker's injuries, attempting to hide his uneasiness in vain. The girls spoke with short, quick instructions to one another. Tension hung in the air like a dense fog.

The meal eaten, utensils cleaned, Hihn and Kahla rolled out their bedding under the wagon. Rachel lit a lantern and climbed into the wagon to re-arrange her blankets beside Stryker. She set Stryker's clothing aside but laid his pants near him in case he awoke. No use aggravating his injuries now. He could get dressed or be dressed if he regained consciousness.

Rachel undressed and pulled out her nightgown, and then she froze, clutching the garment to her bosom.

"*Buenos noches*." The guttural accent of the Mexican interrupted the bed, making chatter between Hihn and Kahla.

Hihn, started to reach for his Winchester, but two carbines were already pointed at him. He crawled from under the wagon without a weapon and stood between the men and Kahla, who stayed hidden beneath her blanket.

"What you want?" Hihn asked.

"The 'orse and monies. Then we go." The second Mexican kept his gun aimed at Hihn and shuffled backward to the rear of the Conestoga, while his partner stayed with Hihn.

Rachel's first reaction was to drop the nightgown and grab her clothing instead of reaching for the shotgun. She regretted not going for the gun.

"*Señorita*, you make ready for Ernesto, *si?*" Ernesto glanced quickly at Stryker and saw the heavily bandaged man was not moving. "Your *hombre* ees bad hurt? He won't mind if Ernesto takes his place. Maybe you like better, *si?*"

"Ernesto?" The Mexican by Hihn started to get nervous.

"Raul, the *señorita* has undressed. She begs for me." Ernesto held onto the carbine and climbed in the wagon.

Rachel dropped her clothes and reached for the shotgun. Ernesto lunged forward, driving into her chest, and the scattergun flew from her hands. He gripped Rachel's throat and pinned her to the floor, sitting on her chest. He shoved the shotgun to the front of the wagon. Rachel struggled to breathe, but Ernesto tightened his grip. Just as she began to pass out, he loosened it, and she managed to suck in a ragged breath before he slammed his fist into the side of her head.

"Now, maybe you like Ernesto to fuck you, *si?*" He raised his fist.

Rachel attempted to speak, but she could only cough.

"*Si?*"

Rachel nodded weakly.

"*Bueno.*" Ernesto unbuckled the gun belt and worked his pants down his hips. "When we finish, you will tell all your *amigos* how Ernesto make love to you."

"Rachel?" Hihn started for the back of the wagon. "Leave her alone you . . .!" The barrel of Raul's carbine whacked hard against his ear and he went down to all fours.

"*Señor*, you have business with Raul. Monee and the 'orse. First, the money *por favor.*

"In *der* other wagon." Hihn struggled to his feet.

"*Bueno.*" Raul jabbed the end of the barrel into Hihn's back and pushed him forward.

Ernesto spread Rachel's knees and fell on top, smashing his chest against hers. He pinned her wrists over her head to the wagon floor and then used his left hand to hold both. With the other hand, he guided his manhood inside. He began to pump, then harder, and with each stroke he grunted, spraying Rachel's face with spittle.

"*Dios mio*! *Yo soy . . .*" The exclamation ended in a gurgle.

The razor entered Ernesto's neck just below his ear. The tender skin parted easily, and the crimson gap grew wider as the blade traveled across his throat. Blood gushed onto Rachel's chest and the Mexican's face quietly settled between her blood-soaked breasts. She felt the warm liquid flowing on her upper torso, but she didn't realize it was blood until Ernesto's body slid to her side. Then, before she could scream, she saw Stryker's arm lying on her chest; the razor slipping from his fingers.

Rachel dropped her hands onto the floorboard to move away from the two men. Blood draped her chest in a dark coat and down her ribs to the floor. Choking back another scream, she pressed her palms on the boards and pushed, but her hands slipped in the blood. She pursed her lips, clenched her teeth, and shoved her feet. Her head banged against the shotgun.

"Ernesto, I got the money! Get the 'orse. *Vamanos*!" Raul held the small box in the air and ran to the Conestoga. "Ernesto! *Vamanos*! *Vamanos*! Look! We're rich!" Raul looked inside the wagon and held up the box to show Ernesto. His eyes were slow to adjust.

The 12-gauge roared and jumped skyward from Rachel's slickened fingers. Raul took the blast one inch below the brim of his sombrero. With his scalp blown away, Raul stumbled backward and crumbled to the ground.

Hihn had stayed by the freight wagon. The Winchester lay under the buckboard. His decision-making cut short by the shotgun. He whirled to see Raul fall, with shreds of the sombrero landing several feet behind him.

"Rachel!" Kahla yelled. Peering out from under her blanket, she watched Raul hit the ground.

"Rachel!" Hihn bellowed.

"I'm, I'm, all right. They're dead."

Hihn ran to the wagon, jumping over Raul's legs as he ran. Kahla scrambled from under the Conestoga and the two of them looked over the tailgate.

When Kahla saw Rachel, she screamed. "Rachel!"

Rachel threw away the shotgun and grabbed Stryker's shirt to cover her bloodied chest. "Help me clean up this mess and get him," pointing to Ernesto, "out of here." Her voice wavered, but she collected herself.

"What happened?" Kahla asked.

"Stryker killed him. I don't know how, but he did. Now his head's bleeding again. Pull the Mexican out and wipe up the blood. I've got to tend to Stryker." Rachel turned and wiped off her chest with the shirt, then found her own and put it on.

Hihn dropped the tailgate and dragged the Mexican out. Then he pulled both bodies several hundred feet away from the wagons with a mule. When he returned, the women had scoured the wagon floor with hot soapy water. They covered the stained boards with a tarp and decided to let them dry out the next day.

"The moon's up. I'll hitch the mules and take us out of here. We can bed down somewhere else."

Later on the buckboard, Kahla said, "I saw the razor."

"I hope I don't get pregnant." Rachel said.

"You mean that Mexican . . .?"

"Yes, just when Stryker cut his God-damned throat."

"Ha, he came and went at the same time." Kahla grinned at her sister. "And, you satisfied both."

"I never touched the other one." Rachel bit back angrily.

"You blew him to paradise."

CHAPTER FIVE

In spite of Hihn's intentions, the wagons rolled out of camp two hours after sunrise the next morning. However, the road flattened out and they covered the miles at a quickened pace to make up for the delay. Hihn estimated they could still reach Sacramento to meet Hihn's brother, and even Rachel's mood brightened when she got her time of the month, making pregnancy unlikely. And the sun coming out helped as well.

Hihn stopped the wagons early that afternoon to rest and water the mules. Kahla tended to Stryker while Rachel prepared a noon meal out of cured ham and biscuits.

"I didn't wake him. Tried to give him a little water, and he choked," Kahla said, walking from the wagon.

"We should be in town by tomorrow night. If he's alive, a doctor might do him some good," Hihn replied with a mouthful of food. Then, before he bit into the biscuit again, he added, "If we have no more trouble."

Rachel searched Hihn's face for any sign her uncle had more to say on the subject. He didn't.

Hihn rose to his feet. "Let's get on *der* trail." He forced a smile, regretting the remark about trouble.

⚔

Stryker rested in the wagon alone. Since the attack, Rachel preferred to ride up front with her sister, keeping the bloody floorboards out of her sight. Stryker's flirtation with consciousness did not last. An additional loss of blood set back his recovery. But his brain was alive with dreams, some good, some not, some vivid and haunting. Being unconscious provided fertile ground. He usually had nightmares about Leigh and her death. But he never dreamed about men he killed.

Stryker saw a long, dark hallway. He groped his way down, not knowing where it led, feeling along the walls as he went. Suddenly, at the end, a picture flashed on the back wall, bright and vivid. He shielded his eyes. It was Leigh's face, torn and bloody from the exploded artillery shell. She came to life, and with blood bubbling from her mouth, she asked, "Why, Stryker?"

⚔

"Did you hear that?" Kahla asked.

"Hear what?" Rachel snapped the traces.

"I thought he said something."

"When we stop, I'll look for infection or fever." Rachel said.

Hihn drew the freight wagons alongside the Conestoga. "How you girls doing?"

"Do you think we'll be there tomorrow night?" Rachel asked. "I need a hot bath."

"We'll make it. There is about two more hours' daylight. Next water we come to, we *vill* make camp." Hihn slowed his mules and let the girls move ahead. He hadn't meant for them to run into trouble. The reason he'd been willing to pay Stryker's high price was because he had wanted to prevent what happened with the Mexicans. His brother would be no help with a gun. They'd spend a few days in Sacramento, maybe Stryker would recover, or maybe he could find another gun, or guns.

The trail widened, and they began to pass an occasional homestead. A creek sprang up from the ground, but Hihn suspected they were nearing a town and he pushed on. Dusk had fallen by the time they reached Roseville. Unfortunately, the town's flour mill had burned down, and many other buildings were destroyed with it. The two hotels still open had no rooms to let, and with no place to stay, they set up camp west of town. Hihn summoned a doctor for Stryker, but other than cleansing the wounds, the doc said he couldn't do anything more and he suggested getting to Sacramento as soon as possible.

A clear sky welcomed the next morning. The few remaining clouds from the prior day dissipated by dawn and the sun bathed the landscape as soon as it crept over the horizon. Hihn got the mules hitched while the girls prepared breakfast and tended to their morning chores. Their moods were brightened considerably by the cheerful weather and the prospect of warm baths and beds in a hotel.

"Well, girls, I see you move better this morning," Hihn said, coming to the cooking fire for his coffee. "You are looking forward to Sacramento? I am too. How is he?"

Rachel set a small pot near the flames. "His lips were caked and cracked, and I swabbed them with water. He licked his lips, and I kept trying to give him more 'til he started choking again. He never opened his eyes and he wouldn't answer when I said his name. I'm warming some broth. He needs to get something in him."

"Hmmm . . ." Hihn grunted, "maybe he will make it to Sacramento. I think twenty miles and we should get there before dark."

"What are we going to do with him?" Kahla asked.

"Have a doctor see him. Go from there," Hihn replied.

"I mean, where will we put him? You told us we could sleep in a hotel. We can't just leave him in the wagon."

"I think we can use his own money and get him a room too. I am sure not paying for it." Hihn neglected to mention he had agreed to pay Stryker's hotel room in Sacramento, but he reasoned the mixed-breed had not kept his part of the bargain.

Early evening shadows stretched across the trail by the time they rolled into Sacramento from the northeast, their arrival delayed due to the American River crossing. Hihn asked an elderly couple in a passing buggy where he might find a hotel. They told him to try the Ebner Hotel on K Street, between Front and Second streets. The Ebner and its sister hotel, the Empire, turned out to be just a few steps from the Sacramento River Embarcadero where Hihn planned to meet his brother, Renard. Renard and the steam donkey would arrive by barge in four days, and he would help Hihn drive the freight wagons to Felton. The extra time in Sacramento could be used to rest the mules.

Hihn led the wagons through town until they pulled in front of the three-story Ebner Hotel. He instructed the girls to wait with the wagons while he went inside. Ten minutes later, he re-emerged, followed by two husky young men in their late teens. The boys pulled up short by the Conestoga flashing silly grins and stood gawking at Kahla and Rachel. Hihn quickly herded them to the rear of the wagon.

"Back here." Hihn ordered, noting the young men's interest in his nieces. "Make the tailgate down and slide him out. Take him up to room 35. We *vill* be back soon. One of you remain with him until the doctor comes."

"Oowee, what happened to him?" The tow-headed boy called Waylon asked. "He's all torn to hell."

"He flirted with my girls." Hihn snorted.

Waylon gingerly rolled Stryker onto his back and grabbed under his armpits. His buddy, Gil, hooked his arms under Stryker's knees and the two boys dragged him from the wagon. "I don't think that old man could a done this to him," Waylon grunted as they carried the mixed-breed into the hotel.

"Looks like a bear got him." Gil said, fingering the ripped clothing after they'd taken Stryker upstairs and laid him on the bed.

"You can go, I'll stay with him," Gil said without looking up from Stryker.

"That's okay, I'll stay too."

Gil looked at his friend and they both broke out laughing.

"You think one of them girls is his?" Gil's mirthful laugh faded to a frown.

"Look at him. He ain't gonna be doin' much about nothing for a while," Waylon replied, sounding optimistic.

Gil studied the tall man stretched out on the bed, "All the same, if he gets better, I don't want him coming after me."

CHAPTER SIX

Hihn and the girls followed the hotel clerk's directions to the doctor's office, walking three blocks from the river and one block north to the Hotel California where Doc Coblenz used a rented room as his office. A small sign tacked on the hotel corner read "Elijah Coblenz, M.D." with an arrow pointing down the alley. They passed by the stairs to the second story and found a side entrance. His office was the first room on the left, and the sharp smell of rubbing alcohol guided them to the partially closed door.

"Ow, shit, you ole buzzard. That burns like hell." The young cowboy, his pants off, sat on the examining table with one pale leg stretched out in front, his hands gripping the table's edges behind him. His other leg hung to the floor, and it straightened when Coblenz poured the stinging liquid into a nine-inch gash that ran inside the laid-out thigh.

"Aw, quit your whining. I could just let the infection fester and cut the leg off at your balls."

"Don't be doin' no cuttin' around the boys, doc. Them fellers got lots of work ahead of 'em." The cowboy settled back on the table as the pain subsided.

"Excuse me." Hihn's knuckles rapped against the door jamb.

"I'm busy right now," Coblenz said, as he poured more alcohol on the leg.

The cowboy twisted his upper body around, bumping the doctor's hand and causing him to splash extra fluid on the cut. "Damn doc!" He saw the girls and started for his trousers.

"Stay where you are! I'm not finished." Coblenz shoved the cowboy back on the table. He turned to Hihn. "Tell your girls to wait outside." The doctor motioned Hihn out the door with the bottle in his hand.

"When you finish, I got a man over at the Ebner Hotel." Hihn stepped out of the doorway and gently pushed his two nieces down the hall. "You girls go back over to Mister Stryker. We'll be along soon."

Hihn closed the door behind him and stepped outside. He pulled a cigar from his coat pocket, lit it, and leaned against a support post under the stairs. The cigar was half smoked when Coblenz came out with his medical bag.

"I think a grizzly bear attacked him," Hihn said as they started walking.

⤝

Gil and Waylon lingered in Stryker's room after the girls got back, trying to strike up a conversation. That didn't go well. The girl's accents made them laugh. After a few awkward words, they fell silent and stood away from Stryker's bed while Rachel and Kahla fussed with the pillow and linen. The boys took turns elbowing each other in the ribs, attempting to goad one or the other into saying something artful. Before they could mine the right words of apology, Hihn opened the door and came in, followed by Doc Coblenz.

"You two go now. Here is your money." Hihn dug two coins from his vest pocket and dropped one apiece into the outstretched hands of Waylon and Gil.

The two boys stood for a while, trying to decide what to do next, stay or go. Hihn made it easy. He held the door open as Coblenz went to work on Stryker.

"Thank you. If I need you again, I *vill* ask downstairs."

Doctor Coblenz stripped off the bandages and rolled Stryker over from side to side, examining the multiple attack sites. He reapplied new dressings to the more serious wounds and left the lesser ones uncovered.

"Will he be all right? Kahla asked.

"He's lost a lot of blood." Coblenz put his stethoscope, thermometer, and alcohol bottle in his bag. "Try to keep the wounds clean and let me know when, or if, he comes to. Throw that stuff away," he said, pointing to the bloody cloths.

"Somebody owes me two dollars." Coblenz held out an upturned palm.

Hihn picked up Stryker's pants. He dug out the money and slapped it on the doctor's open hand. Coblenz picked up his medical bag and headed for the door.

Rachel and Kahla stayed by Stryker's bed, leaving his room only for their own needs. They swabbed his lips with water and soup broth, being careful not to choke him on the liquids.

Deep in the recesses of Stryker's brain, memories flashed in ragged sequences, performing scenes in his mind as if in a stage play. Some he was in, some not, but he watched them all, seeing himself and others as if they were characters acting out parts. He was always in the background, floating in the shadows, neither standing nor sitting. Just there, watching. The scenes came and went quickly. He drifted back. Leigh, a regular haunt, tormented him the most. Not this time, though. Memories of another brief acquaintance years before Leigh played in this dream.

She'd been nineteen when Stryker met her. Barbara's folks left her when she was seventeen. They moved to another state and never wrote to tell her where they landed, said she was trouble and always would be–in and out of jail for public drunkenness, thievery, and assault against women . . . and men. She led a rowdy life. After her parents left her in Arizona Territory, the only time she slept in a bed was in jail, until Stryker came along. On leave from General Crook's Army and the Indian campaigns, Captain Stryker had elected to spend his free days in the nearest decent sized town, Tucson.

Barbara Ada Langford, her full name, had been in Tucson most of her life. Barbara never owned a skirt. Dressing like a man, she always wore denim pants and a shirt. She wore her closely cropped hair short, and she had a habit of sitting with one leg propped up, resting an elbow on it the way a man does when he's telling a tall tale. Only she never told tales. A fair hand at cards even when she didn't cheat, she hung around saloons hustling unsuspecting cowboys. After she cheated enough or pilfered enough from the tables, she'd go to another watering hole and drink until she passed out.

Many men had tried to bed her. She had a trim figure and an angular, somewhat attractive face, hard, but certainly not ugly. However, sex wasn't part of her life. A lot of the scrapes she had were the result of spurned advances. She carried a knife, and she knew how to use it. She never gave much thought to old age. Her future plans extended as far as the next drink.

The night Barb met Stryker began with a run in, literally. Fleeing from two men she had cheated at cards, she darted down an alley where Stryker had just taken a piss, and he threw his hands against Barb's shoulders preventing a full collision.

"Ooomph! Let me go!" Barb tried to wrench herself free from his grasp.

"There she is!" The first cowboy to round the saloon corner yelled. "She's got a partner too."

Barb managed to spin around to face her pursuers. She backed up to Stryker's side and grabbed his arm with both hands. "Yeah, and you better leave me alone!"

"We don't abide card cheats, even if it's a woman, mister," said the second cowboy, drawing up next to his friend.

"I didn't cheat you. Your luck ain't no good."

"Let go of the arm." Stryker grabbed Barb's wrist and twisted. His strong grip caused her to drop both hands. As soon as she did, he drew and cocked the Peacemaker. His speed was not lost on the two cowboys.

"Easy, mister. Fourteen dollars ain't worth it. C'mon, Bill."

"Why didn't you shoot them?" Barb asked when the cowboys had gone.

"I should have let them beat the shit out of you." He walked out the alley and headed toward the saloon across the street. When he came out two hours later, she was waiting for him. She followed him to a two-room shack a half mile south of town. He'd been renting it while on leave.

Stryker didn't invite her in. She slept outside. For the next several days, he went about his business in town. He was aware of her trailing him, knew she slept outside, but made no effort to approach her, and she kept her distance as well. On the fifth night, he left the door open. Sometime around midnight, she entered and climbed into his bed. She curled up behind his back and they slept.

The next morning Stryker rose, built a fire, and made coffee. She got out of bed and sat on the floor, watching. He went outside and tended to his horse, leaving her inside. Later, he headed to town. She stayed in the shack.

When Stryker returned later in the day, he found the place had been cleaned and scrubbed. She had bathed and brushed her hair. A jar filled with red globemallow flowers sat on the lone table. That night he ate, leaving extra food in the pot which she never touched, and went to bed. Barb followed once she knew he had fallen asleep.

The routine went like that for a week. She always ate when he wasn't around. On Saturday, Stryker bathed in town. That night, instead of waiting for him to fall asleep, Barb went to his bed early. She took off her clothes and straddled him. Later, as she lay behind his bare back, she said, "You don't have to bathe in town. I'll bathe you."

Barbara made coffee the next morning. She made it the following morning too, and she began to prepare the meals. Words remained few. Ten days passed, and he still didn't know the girl's name, nor did she know his.

Once, when two Apaches had called on Stryker and issued a threat, she charged from the side and stuck her knife in the ribs of the closest brave. Stryker was so surprised by the move; he hadn't drawn his gun.

He'd been away for several days. He hadn't told her where he was going or when he would be back. She waited. His clothes left in the shack told her he would return. Six days passed before he did. Normally, she came out to greet him when she heard his approach. Not that day. Barb wasn't in the shack either. Stryker assumed she'd left and gone back to town.

He found her the next morning. She stood naked, tied spread-eagled against the back wall. Her breasts had been cut off.

Since he saw no other wounds, Stryker figured it took two or three days to die. He buried her and rode into town to report her death.

A week later, a cavalry patrol riding twenty miles west of Tucson came across a party of five dead Apaches. They had been shot. Two of them, who may have survived the gunshots, had their arms and legs lashed together around the base of a giant saguaro cactus. They appeared to have been brutally tortured.

⚔

The next five days in Sacramento went the same, the girls nursing Stryker as best they could. On the sixth day, with Hihn's help, the girls pulled him up to a sitting position supported on extra pillows. Kahla held his head steady while Rachel placed a partial spoonful of broth on his lower lip and tilted it so that a little trickled into his mouth. To their relief, Stryker swallowed. Each time after that they were able to gradually increase the servings.

Hihn visited room 35 daily. "Well girls," he said on day nine, "me and Renard are prepared to go. Wagons packed. Tomorrow is Sunday. We *vill* be going Monday morning *vith* or *vithout* him, and he is not coming *vith* us like this." Then he walked out.

The girls got desperate.

"We have to wake him." Rachel was all business. "Let's pull the blankets off, try to get him to feel something." Stryker wore only bandages under the bedding and once uncovered, his physique revealed his fitness. Even after seeing his body several times over the past nine days, Kahla's face still turned crimson and her eyes widened with approval. Rachel ignored his nakedness. She gripped his bicep with both hands and shook. "Stryker, wake up!"

Kahla went around the bed and sat on Stryker's opposite side. She followed her sister's lead with his other arm. "C'mon, Stryker!"

Rachel bent to his ear. "You have to wake up. We need you." Sitting up straight, she said, "We've got to do more."

Deep inside Stryker's brain, flashes of past scenes began mixing with physical sensations of the present.

Stryker's eyelids fluttered, his mind alive with vivid images-two saloon girls . . . wallpapered room above the Bucket of Blood saloon . . . Virginia City . . . feeling very drunk.

"I think he's coming around." Rachel said anxiously.

He sensed pleasure . . . *intense* pleasure. "Easy girls . . . whoa . . . honey . . . stop damn it." He tried to tell them, but his mouth wouldn't form the words.

"What's he saying?" Rachel asked.

"Don't know. Mumbling something though."

"Wake up, cowboy. Hurry it, Kahla," Rachel urged.

"Kahla . . . in Virginia City?" Stryker started breaking through.

"Can't hold it! Shit!" Stryker said out loud and he felt himself release a series of eruptions. He blinked several times, as his eyes opened for the first time since the grizzly attack. He looked down at his groin where Kahla still milked his stiff rod and Rachel was using a towel to clean things.

"We decided to give you a hand," Kahla laughed, more excited about Stryker regaining consciousness than her own wit.

"How long . . . has . . . it been?" Stryker struggled to make sense of what just happened.

"You tell us, cowboy. But, by the looks of things, quite a while," Kahla giggled.

"Nine days," Rachel told him. "That bear nearly killed you."

"Bear?"

CHAPTER SEVEN

Stryker lifted his head off the pillow. Bracing on one elbow, he tried to swing his legs onto the floor, but Rachel shoved them back on the bed.

"Not yet! You're too weak," Rachel ordered. She pulled the sheet under Stryker's chin.

"Clothes." Stryker looked around the room. Rachel sat on the bed, blocking his view of a straight-back chair with brown paper packages neatly stacked on it. On top of the packages lay the Peacemaker with the gun belt, his razor, and the sai resting on a stack of cash.

"We pulled a shirt from your saddlebags," Rachel said. "Uncle Hihn used your money to buy you a coat and pair of pants, and I don't know what else. He said if you didn't wake up, they could bury you in them."

Stryker lay back and ran his hand over the swollen ridges on his scalp. "Where the hell am I?"

"You're in Sacramento," Kahla answered, moving closer to the bed, where she stood beside him. She had picked up the sai and examined it, like she had many times before. "We've all been wondering. What is this? It was stuck in your pants, so it has to be . . ."

"Mine."

"But what is it?" Kahla asked again.

"I need to eat." Stryker said to Rachel.

During the doctor's last visit, he'd said Stryker needed another seven days. Hihn visited Stryker again on Sunday and had his doubts about him being ready before that. But then, despite trepidations otherwise, the mixed-breed saddled the roan early Monday morning.

Stryker led the big horse out of the livery and stood it next to the corral. He climbed two rails, got a boot in the stirrup, and eased his body into the saddle. Hihn and his brother were tying sections of the steam donkey on the freight wagons when he rode up.

"Morning." Hihn offered the greeting without cheer, but its simplicity conveyed business as usual. When Stryker made no move to dismount, Hihn did introductions while he pulled on the rope. "This is Stryker. He's Renard." Hihn stopped with the tie-down and looked at his brother. "We *vill* need him."

Hihn's brother could have been his twin, but they were actually six years apart in age, Renard being junior. Throughout their lives, Renard never could catch up to his older sibling and continued to take orders from Hihn. Stryker leaned forward in the saddle, easing weight off his backside, and observed Renard work the ropes. *You can tell a lot about a man by his hands*, Stryker thought. Strong hands, weak hands, gentle hands, steady hands, and nervous hands. Renard had nervous hands. They shook badly. He shivered like a man with the chills. But he didn't have the chills. A drunk, maybe. He had a hard time looping a knot. When he noticed Stryker watching him, he got even more nervous and turned his body to shield his rope tying from the man on the horse.

Hihn secured the ropes on his side of the wagon and came around to help his brother. Renard stepped back and allowed Hihn to finish tying down the wagon. After watching Hihn work for a few minutes, he glanced past his brother and got a good look at Stryker. Renard averted his eyes when Stryker returned his gaze.

Renard drove the first freight wagon, Rachel and Kala sat in the Conestoga, and Hihn brought up the second freight wagon, hauling most of the disassembled steam donkey. Stryker rode on ahead.

The sun had climbed to high noon when Renard led the wagons to shade under a large oak tree and by a narrow creek. Still early spring, the sparsely leafed oak and flat lowlands afforded little shelter from the heat of the day. He and Hihn unhitched the freight wagons.

"We ought to make Lodi by tomorrow," Hihn said, pulling the mules forward. "Cannot get there today. There are small settlements by Lodi on *der* Mokelumne River and I want to be a little time there." Hihn lifted his arms to help Rachel and Kahla off the Conestoga. "They float logs down *der* river during spring to a steam engine mill. Men there told me they could do 40,000 feet a day. It is not *der* same engine we have, but me and Renard plan to use *der* steam donkey to haul out them logs."

Stryker saw the wagons pull off the trail and spurred the roan to a canter. He'd always been a lean man, but now he looked gaunt and tired. Though he rode straight in the saddle, his bones punched through the skin.

Hihn watched him ride up to the wagons and dismount with no outward signs of fatigue, and he allowed the gunman his respect. "We *vill* rest and water *die* mules." Hihn unhitched the Conestoga's team and led the mules behind Renard and the other two teams, to the creek. Stryker brought the roan several feet upstream and let it draw the cold, clear water. After a few short minutes, he gave the reins a sharp tug, pulling its muzzle from the creek.

"So," Hihn continued, "me and Renard *vill* go inspect *die* mill after arriving to town. Stryker, keep *die* girls safe until we get back. Lodi's a nice town and you can look around while we are gone. Later, we *vill* make a list and get supplies we need."

Stryker figured Hihn remained unaware of the nieces' handiwork and simply nodded. His weakened condition put him in a bad mood. But then, he was always in a bad mood. It would be at least two weeks before he fully regained his strength. In the meantime, vulnerability would ride with him.

CHAPTER EIGHT

Hihn gave up on getting to Lodi the next day. By the time they forded the Cosumnes and Dry Rivers, the sun had dropped behind the tree-covered hills to the west. Continuing south, they reached the steeply wooded banks that collared the much larger Mokelumne River, seasonally swollen from spring runoff, and decided to make camp on its north side. Twilight was fading fast and Lodi, some three-fourths of a mile beyond the south fork, would have to wait another day.

Stryker chose not to eat with the others. Grabbing a plate and a mug of coffee, he wandered off to sit near the river. The women cooked well, different but tasty meals, and they brewed coffee strong, the way he liked it. A cool breeze sweeping across the river brought a slight chill that went well with the hot coffee. He sat and ate, letting thoughts or memories flow through his head like the river before him.

"There he goes again." Rachel said, as she sat by the cook fire with Kahla and her uncles. "I believe he doesn't like our company. You'd think he'd be a little more grateful or talkative, seeing as how we saved his life."

"Man has right to his thoughts," Hihn offered, before he forked down a mouthful of runza.

"Men like him are better left alone," Renard grunted.

"Maybe he doesn't like a crowd. Maybe he'll talk to just one." Kahla stared absently after Stryker. It'd turned dark and all she could see was the black void beyond the reaches of the flickering firelight. The night swallowed him, or perhaps welcomed him into its darkness.

"One . . . like you, Kahla?" Rachel asked. Her words bore a dusting of jealousy.

"He's wrestling with angels," Kahla said wistfully.

"Angels would not go near him." Hihn brought the beef pocket to his mouth, then dropped it down. "That man is in in savage fight *vith der* devil, and I feel sorry for *der* devil."

Kahla sat her plate down, rose, and moved briskly around the men and Rachel, slowing when she got out of the firelight. She brushed her clothing with her hands and slipped the scarf from her hair.

"Fool girl," Hihn growled. Rachel and Renard went back to their runzas, content to let Kahla learn a lesson with the mixed-breed on her own.

Stryker saw Kahla's figure step away from the campfire, coming his way. He stayed seated on the log he'd found on the river bank and he turned back to watch the dark water silently rushing by, eating, and listening to Kahla stumbling in his direction.

"Mister Stryker, there you are. Why you out here by yourself? Don't like us?" He didn't answer, but she sat down next to him, anyway. "Ever been married?"

"Wife's dead. Gotta shit." He got up, left the plate and cup on the log, and walked off.

"How'd it go?" Rachel asked, somewhat amused Kahla returned so quickly.

"I asked if he'd been married. He said she was dead and then informed me he had to go execute a bowel movement. That ended our talk."

"Married, huh?" Rachel said, cocking her head pensively. "Hard to imagine. Well, it's bedtime."

"Hey! You girls going to sleep all day?" Hihn already had a team of mules hitched to one of the freight wagons. His angry bellow split the early morning chill. Hihn seemed irritated his working the mules hadn't roused the others. Stryker, though, was already up, and he'd ridden ahead in the gray morning light to scout the trail.

"Hihny, waking the cock this morning," Kahla complained inside the Conestoga.

"He wants to see that damn sawmill." Rachel threw her nightgown toward a drawer she couldn't see. "Better get out there. Smells like he's got a fire started, and I need something hot before we start out."

"Good morning, girls." Hihn's mood improved now that everyone had joined him. "Once we get across and in town, you *vill* be free to rest, or eat, or whatever you like. Just stay away from trouble."

"Make me some coffee!" Renard yelled from where he was urinating in the trees. The younger German's accent was not as thick as his brother's.

Stryker and the roan came back, appearing out of the fog. "Want some coffee Stryker?" Rachel pulled the coffeepot from the grate, filled a cup, and held it out to him. He dismounted and approached the cook fire. "Water's not too deep. We can get across. Footing's good." Stryker reached for the offered cup.

"You want me to take the lead wagon?" Renard asked, bringing up another team of mules.

"Yes, girls next, then me," Hihn answered. "Mister Stryker, if you would cross ahead of Renard, we would be grateful." He added.

Stryker's replied with a barely perceptible nod.

Stryker's judgment proved solid. The river rose no higher than the wheel hubs. He entered town ahead of the wagons, located the Lodi Livery, and waited outside while the stable hand took care of the roan. Ten minutes later, the Hihn's arrived in Lodi, population 800, and rolled by trees sprouting buds soon to provide shade, planted in neat rows lining the streets. They rode down a long row of freshly painted wooden buildings, a butcher shop, hardware, and jewelry stores on Sacramento Street. The drug and jewelry fronts adorned with colorful signs, welcomed visitors. The butcher shop, hardware, and mill had different placards, but the buildings looked new and their sidewalks were swept clean. Once Stryker saw the Hihn wagons heading for the stable, he went inside. There, he met with the blacksmith to get the big horse re-shod, carefully inspecting each hoof with the farrier to ensure a proper fit.

Renard and Hihn unhitched the teams, then paid the stable hand to water and feed the mules. Rachel and Kahla waited outside, having decided not to insult their senses with the foul-smelling interior. They took turns peeking through the open door, watching for their uncles. The two men eventually came out and met with the girls. "See if we can rent a couple of rooms. We'll stay the night and leave in the morning," Hihn said to Rachel.

"What about Stryker? Rachel asked.

"He can stay *vith* me and Renard or someplace else. He can decide." Hihn didn't see Kahla's foot nudge Rachel's.

"Kahla and me'll explore the town. We rode by a hotel called Sargent House, looked clean and new from the outside. We'd like to stay there!" Rachel chirped. Hihn nodded. "When will you be back and where should we meet?" Rachel asked with growing elation and ignored another Kahla foot thump.

Stryker came out of the stable, carrying a small valise and the carbine. He set the bag on the ground, canted the gun barrel on his shoulder, and leaned against the wall, listening to the conversation.

"Early afternoon, suppertime, I have to inventory mill equipment and take measurements, make notes and drawings. Stryker, won't be needed so he can stay in town. Watch you two," Hihn said. He glanced at the mixed-breed, who offered no sign of not accepting the charge.

Hihn had had enough of mule riding, so he and Renard re-entered the stable and rented horses for the ride to the Lodi Land and Saw Mill. Lodi built the logging mill away from town. However, another mill, the planing mill, sat at the far end of Sacramento Street. Rachel and Kahla swirled to face each other, exchanged flashing grins of excitement, and started for the Sargent Hotel with a jump and two skips. Stryker trailed behind the nieces, content to let them speed ahead. However, they soon separated and slowed, each hooking an arm with his. Two of three faces wore broad smiles.

Rachel and Kahla stopped at the hotel desk. Stryker went on to the dining room for steak and eggs. After securing the rooms and having their slat trunks delivered, the girls met up with Stryker in the dining room.

"Uncle Hihny just wanted two rooms, one for me and Kahla, one for the men." Rachel said, sitting down with her sister at Stryker's table. "He told me he just agreed to get you a room in Sacramento and that this would do"

"If you don't want to sleep . . ." Kahla started to say.

"I'll find my own place." Stryker said as he cut the steak.

Rachel muttered something in German and Kahla burst out laughing.

Stryker looked up from his plate and squinted at Rachel.

Kahla, still laughing, said, "Well, if you want to know what she said . . ."

Stryker turned to Kahla.

"She said," Kahla continued, "if you're gonna act like a turd, go lay in the yard."

"Kahla and I have asked for more things to be brought to our room." Rachel said, with a hint of a smile directed at Stryker. She got no reaction. "Come on, sister, we'll have to pick out what to bring up." They left Stryker to his steak and eggs.

"He's sure a hard man to get to know." Rachel said.

The girls eyed each other, and their laughter began anew.

Stryker was on his second cup of coffee and still in the dining room when the girls stopped by to say they planned a walk through town. After grabbing sweet rolls at a bakery if they found one, they'd stroll around. He topped off his cup, walked outside, took a seat on a wooden chair in front of the hotel, and leaned it back against the wall. Sipping his coffee, he watched them enter Hanson's Drug Store, cross the street, and come out later with a bag of what appeared to be pastries. Then they wandered into Hill's Jewelry Store.

"Fire! Fire! Fire at the mill!"

Stryker looked down Sacramento Street and saw a man in denim overalls waving his arms as he ran. Farther down, he saw heavy black smoke billowing out behind the running man and flames shooting above the Novelty Planing Mill. Within seconds, the fire arced over the wooden roof and spread to the next building. Driving winds fanned what quickly became a blazing inferno to the third wooden structure, and the sound of the fire went from barely noticeable to a thunderous roar.

With no break between the tinder boxes of wooden buildings, Stryker surmised it would only take a few minutes for the jewelry store to be engulfed in flames. Suddenly the store's front door flew open. A short, bare-headed, middle-aged man wearing a gray suit came out. He looked up the street, then faced the opposite direction and saw the fire coming his way. Stryker expected him to yell a warning for those inside. Instead, he ran back in and slammed the door.

Stryker took one last gulp of coffee, pushed the chair legs down with a thud, and set the cup by the chair. He made his way across the street, letting other townsfolk who rushed outside dodge around him. The door to Hill's was locked. He banged his fist on the heavy front door. No answer. He quick stepped along the building front, jumped off the boarded sidewalk with one long hop, and ran down the narrow alleyway to the back.

Intense smoke, drifting toward the store, made it difficult to see and breathe. No flames had yet reached the building, or the one next to it, but he saw wisps of smoke curling away from two nearby wooden structures and he knew he had only seconds to find the girls.

There, in the rear doorway, he met up with the little man furiously pushing on a wheelbarrow loaded with colorful display boxes. The wheelbarrow had wedged itself tightly against both doorjambs and wouldn't budge. Stryker grabbed the front of the bucket and shoved it backward. He then canted the wheelbarrow and pulled it through the door, along with the man still gripping the handles.

"The two girls!" Stryker shouted, as the storekeeper tried swerving the wheelbarrow around him.

"Got to get my jewelry out! What ain't stolen'll burn!" The jeweler drove the wheelbarrow toward a one-horse wagon and started throwing boxes on it.

Stryker leaped through the door.

"Hey! You can't go in there!" The store keeper threw an armful of boxes over the sideboard and scurried after him.

Inside, Stryker found what appeared to be the storeroom. Smoke began filtering into the cramped room, but with the exception of a desk, an open safe, and several closed cabinets, it was empty. A door on the opposite wall appeared to lead to the street-side display room. He side-stepped the desk and tried the door. Locked.

"Get out of here!" The jeweler darted up behind Stryker, grabbed an arm with both hands, and pulled.

"Unlock that door." Stryker demanded, ignoring the little man's grip.

"It must have blown shut and locked!" Yanking harder, the jeweler's voice rose higher, "Don't know where the key is. You get out!"

Stryker throttled the smaller man's throat and swung him about, slamming him against the locked door. "Open it!"

"Please . . ." the choked man spat a desperate plea. Some of the spit dribbled down his chin.

Stryker released his grip, crouched, and drove his shoulder into the jeweler's mid-section. Both men crashed through the door and landed on the floor of the salesroom. Stryker sprang to his feet; smoke burned his eyes, making it hard to see. He bolted past the counter, quickly searching the room. No girls.

The wind had been knocked out of the storekeeper, who rolled to all fours, struggling to catch his breath. He managed to crawl toward the front door, still gasping for air, and clawed at the doorknob.

Stryker, right behind, undid the bolt latch, and banged the door open against the jeweler's head. He snatched the back of the man's belt and heaved him out of his way through the door.

"Look, a stranger saved Mister Hill!" A man pointed and shouted from the gathering street crowd.

Stryker looked past that man, and saw the Hihn brothers leading skittish horses, with Kahla and Rachel walking behind them.

CHAPTER NINE

Hihn broke into a clumsy jog, leading the horses along the far side of Sacramento Street, and away from the roaring fire. Stryker made for the stable. The brothers caught up with him, one on each side, working hard to match his pace. Rachel and Kahla fell in behind.

"Hey, Stryker, why were they pointing?" Kahla shouted above the inferno.

"I'd say they mistook him for someone he's not," Rachel yelled back, her eyes locked on Stryker marching ahead. "Hey, where we going?"

"We are not staying here tonight." Hihn barked. "The whole town *vill* burn down."

Rachel stopped. "We need to get our things from the hotel!"

"Stryker, me and Renard *vill* turn in *die* horses an' get *die* mules. *Vill* get your horse too. Meet you behind *der* stable where we left *die* wagons. Help the fräuleins get their things from *das* hotel."

"I'm not good with the mules," Renard complained to Stryker. When he saw his scowl, he added under his breath, "and you're just as stubborn."

"I'll watch the town burn in front of the hotel," Stryker growled.

He took off for Sergeant's. The girls ran past him and up the hotel steps, leaping the three steps in two.

A bucket brigade began forming as men, women, and children big enough to carry a pail, scrambled into a line from the street well to the flames. A portly man shouted orders above the fire's roar to bring buckets from the hardware store while two other men divided the line. One line snaked to the burning barber shop, the other to the adjacent structure, already smoking on one side.

"We'll have to carry our own damn trunks!" Rachel shouted breathlessly. They raced up the second-floor stairs and reached the room at the same time.

"Drag 'em." Kahla snatched her bag and grasped the trunk handle with her free hand.

Two boys abandoned the fire line and helped the young fräuleins down the front steps . . . as Stryker finished his coffee. By the time they rounded the livery in back, the Hihn brothers had hitched mules to the Conestoga. "Your saddle and gear are on a stall gate." Renard said to Stryker. "We ain't going far, over by those scrub trees and the creek." He nodded toward a clump of Holly a quarter mile away. Got to pick up a few supplies in the mornin' if the hardware store's still standing."

Stryker inspected the roan's hooves and saw that the blacksmith was as good as his word. He went back in for the saddle.

"What you tell hotel man?" Hihn asked no one in particular. He backed a team of mules to one of the freight wagons. "You got that one?" Hihn referred that question to Renard about the other freighter. Not waiting for Renard, Hihn moved on to his niece. "Rachel! You get money back?"

"No! No one at the desk! We just got our own things and left!" Rachel snapped the reins on the mules.

"Well, he's got enough trouble. I *vill* not ask about four dollars."

Hihn and Renard took a freight wagon back into town the next morning and discovered the fire blackened only one side of Sacramento Street, between Pine and Elm. The hardware store remained standing and undamaged, but most of the inventory was gone and the owner refused to sell them what remained.

Hihn and his brother drove the wagon back to Stryker and the girls waiting by the cook fire. Hihn explained why they brought no supplies. "Told us we were from out of town and local folks came first. Reckon I can't blame them." He refilled his cup and swirled the fresh coffee with leftover residue from breakfast. "Stockton just a day more. We *vill* have to get supplies there. I don't remember much between Stockton and Livermore, but it is three more days and on a rutted road. I was hoping we could use rails by now, but they are working on them, switching narrow gauge to standard ones. After Livermore, we *vill* cross coastal hills, then on to San Jose. Surely, we can load freight and donkey on a train there and take it to Felton." Renard stood next to his brother, nodding his agreement.

Stryker mounted the roan and spurred it to an easy gait, heading south. A few minutes later, the three wagons followed.

Due to the late start leaving Lodi, the wagons were unable to reach Stockton before the sun sank, and Hihn begrudgingly stopped four miles outside town. Renard unhitched the mules, and the two women had a cooking fire heating the stew and coffee by the time Stryker rode into camp. He pulled the saddle, hobbled the roan, and grabbed a cup before joining the others by the fire. He poured his own coffee.

It was the first time in almost two weeks since the four-now five, travelers sat to eat together.

"Stryker," Hihn started. "I ought to tell you we may be heading into trouble in San Jose, if not before. Lumber men who haul out them logs got word of *der* steam donkey and they are not happy 'bout losing their jobs. Not only my own crew, other logger outfits *vill* want to bring in one of these critters too. This one's *der* first. If they do not stop me, there *vill* be more," he warned.

Stryker pushed another pile of beans onto his spoon.

"Then there's these agitators, outsiders, come in to stir things up more," Renard added. "They give speeches and get the men all hostiled an' such. Got the loggers gangin' up to do what they call a strike. They stop workin' and try to stop everybody else too. A lot of 'em mad and they figure they'll have more clout acting all together."

"I can understand them being upset." Hihn jumped back in. "But what are you supposed to do, just keep working same old way? If men like these men had their way, we would be digging out log roads with spoons. Besides, other men *vill* have jobs to make *die* donkeys. And yes . . . someday they *vill* lose their jobs too. Something else *vill* come along and replace *der* donkey, something even better. There *vill* be jobs making it too, probably better ones, better jobs than haulin' them logs with ox and men. But these people do not know it that way. So, they aim to stop us. Blood *vill* be flowing."

"Got men to help?" Stryker finally showed interest.

"Few. Outnumbered ten to one." Hihn replied.

"Who's the right man to kill?"

"Stryker, you cannot just go killin' people."

"Said blood'll be spilled. Who needs to bleed?"

Hihn looked at Renard and then cleared his throat. "Well, who is doing *der* most talking is new fellow called Ekard, Heyman Ekard. He is *der* one telling men they ought to revolt, stop us from eliminating their jobs. He said *der* steam donkey is devil's work, has to be destroyed. There have already been killings. I think he is cause of them. Ekard not only one, though. He brought several outsiders in *vith* 'em." Hihn paused, then added, "Do not know if other owners *vill* stand up to him though."

Stryker lowered his cup, swirled the coffee around to pick up the dregs, and emptied the contents on the ground. "Why's that?"

"You want more?" Rachel asked Stryker, offering the coffee pot. "I drained the grounds."

Stryker held out his cup and kept his eyes on Hihn while Rachel re-filled it.

Hihn extended his cup as well. "I cut white pines. They cut big trees, *die* redwoods. No donkey big enough to haul out one of them monsters. They have to saw them and haul out *vith* oxen. They ain't joined *der* strike yet."

"Better." Stryker saluted Rachel with his cup. He'd edged closer to admiration for the German.

Conversation dwindled. One by one, each left the fire to bed down for the night. Stryker left last.

The three wagons pulled into Stockton the next morning. Although the gold mining rush petered out by 1855, the town flourished with diversified industries, the most successful being agriculture. A variety of fruits and vegetables, along with wine, had become important sources of commerce. The Western Pacific Railroad brought rail service to Stockton in 1869, supplanting much of the river traffic, and the town of several thousand was fast becoming one of the most commercialized communities in California.

Hihn drove the lead wagon down El Dorado Street on the way to the waterfront. After passing Fremont Street, he pulled over next to the boardwalk, and in front of Todd's Supply Store. Rachel and Kahla inquired about the Yosemite House while their uncles bought supplies. They found the hotel to their liking; however, the men loaded new provisions by mid-morning and Hihn insisted they push on.

"Hihny," Kahla started. "We were supposed to stop in Lodi, and Stockton is the last decent town before San Jose. You already said there's not much between here and Livermore or San Jose." She folded her arms across her chest and put on her best pout.

"We have to get guards for *die* wagons. Have everything on them." Hihn argued with less conviction than he wanted.

"Stryker can guard them. We're sure paying him enough," Renard offered, siding with Kahla. He glanced at Stryker adjusting the roan's saddle and then whispered loud enough for Hihn to overhear. "Forty a day. What the hell was Hans thinking?"

Night duty swung the debate in favor of the hotel. Hihn resented Stryker's high fee too, and having him guard wagons at night would help justify the extra money. Besides, stationing Stryker by the wagons eliminated the prospect of paying for an extra room or giving an awkward no to a man who slit men's throats. So, the German changed his mind. "Where is *der* hotel?"

"Center and Main Street, couple blocks that way." Rachel pointed with her forefinger.

After hearing Renard's remarks, Stryker fixed a cold eye on him and made a mental note—if Renard ever needed his ass saved, he'd be sure to *help*. "Pull the wagons around back where they can be guarded," Stryker ordered, still staring down the uncle. "Renard, you can watch them when I go eat."

Renard thought about objecting, but a glance at Stryker and he decided against it. "Okay."

They drove the wagons behind the Yosemite Hotel where they unharnessed the mules and tethered them on a rope line strung along feed and water troughs provided for guests. Having Stryker guard the wagons also saved the cost of leaving the animals at a livery. Hihn, pleased with the overall savings, rented a buggy and the Hihn family toured the town for three hours. The driver took them to the waterfront where they'd bought supplies earlier and then drove on to Hunter Square.

Stryker used the time grooming the roan and mending leather. By the time the Hihns returned, he'd worked up an appetite and a thirst only a cold beer could quench. As soon as the buggy rounded into sight at the far end of the backstreet, he pulled a clean shirt from the saddlebag and left to track down food and drink. He chose not to eat at the Yosemite and opted instead for the Occidental Hotel down the street.

A crowded dining room meant a wait for dinner. It was hard to judge whether the aroma of hot food, or the loud talking, or the clatter of plates ruled the room. All three hit the senses about the same. Stryker inquired about a bath at the bar and downed a beer while waiting for a table. One by the window that normally seated four became available, and he headed for it. A gentleman in a pale blue suit and two very attractive, beautifully dressed southern belles, all who'd arrived on the riverboat, got to the table at the same time as Stryker.

"Sir, if you please . . ." said the man, as he smoothly sailed his arms around the women and guided them forward.

The mixed-breed scraped a chair back and sat, leaving the surprised trio to look elsewhere. Stryker waved a young woman wearing an apron over to his table and ordered steak and coffee. The coffee proved weaker than the camp coffee he strained through his teeth, and he'd downed half of the second cup by the time the steak and the woman appeared.

She held her purse in front of her waist with two white-gloved hands, walking hesitantly between tables, looking for someone she knew or a friendly face. The bonnet, the gray, matronly ankle-length dress, and black buckled shoes, made her appear older than her thirty-five years. She came up behind Stryker and his three vacant chairs.

"May I share your table, sir?"

When she came around to Stryker's front, she changed her mind. "Sorry." She recoiled back in shocked surprise. "I . . . I . . . thought . . ."

He lifted his face. His pale eyes locked on to hers. "Sit."

She sat.

Stryker cut into the steak, took a bite. He briefly glimpsed at the woman before looking out the window.

She studied him as he ate and waited until he raised the fork a second time. "You're the hardest looking man I've ever seen." She sat so straight, so poised, the small of her arched spine was four inches from the back of the chair. Her gloved hands clutched the purse in her lap. She cocked an eyebrow, expecting some kind of response. It never came. Stryker peppered the steak.

"We have a grilled chicken special tonight." The waitress had returned unnoticed. "May I take your order, ma'am?"

"The special will do," the woman said. Returning her attention to Stryker, "My name is Agnes, Agnes Kingsley. I'm Mrs. Kingston T. Kingsley."

"Stryker."

"I'm attending the theatre tonight. That's why I'm in a hurry. The

Avon Theatre, Shakespeare's *Twelfth Night*. Lilian Lamson as Viola. Otherwise . . . I wouldn't have sat down . . ."

He made another cut into the steak.

"Are you going? Should be a delightful performance."

"Guarding wagons at Yosemite Hotel," Stryker said between bites.

"You're not from Stockton?" she asked.

Getting no answer, she asked again, "Where are you from?"

"You're not very talkative, Mr. Stryker," Agnes said, impatiently.

"If you want it up the ass, just say so." Stryker growled, as he stabbed a piece of steak with his fork.

"Wha . . . why you crude, vulgar man!"

"The 'hotel special' ma'am." The waitress set the plate in front of Agnes.

Agnes glared at Stryker. However, the chicken looked delicious, and it kept her from jumping up with indignation and marching off in a mad huff. Stryker continued to eat. She watched. She scowled. The chicken beckoned. However, her clenched fists remained under the table. She merely sat, fuming. She noticed how he cut the steak, how he transferred the fork with each bite, and how he made liberal use of the napkin. He'd almost finished the steak when the young page arrived. "Thank goodness," she thought. "Awful man."

"Sir, your bath is ready," the page said.

Stryker downed the last of the coffee. He grabbed the extra shirt under his chair and rose to leave. "Evening."

Agnes waited for him to walk away before she addressed the chicken.

✗

Renard paced around the wagons, waiting for Stryker's return. Renard opted not to rile him and a brief salutation was close enough to the edge. "Good evening, Mister Stryker, and good night."

Stryker inspected the freight wagons and then climbed into the Conestoga and lit a lamp. The makeshift bed the girls used would do. No sleeping on the ground tonight. Spending the night on the hard ground while the rest slept in soft beds, didn't sit well with him. It wasn't the beds themselves; in fact, he preferred the ground. He would also be a better watchman under the wagon. No, he just didn't like being relegated to hired help status.

Stockton had installed gas lamps on the main streets; however, the alleys and back streets remained dark. Stryker arranged the bedding to his liking and climbed out, bringing the lantern. He made one more inspection around the freight wagons and tied the canopy tarp two inches above the side rails on the Conestoga. He re-entered the wagon, checked the field of vision under the canopy, and took off his gun belt, laying it beside him. Settling back on the quilts, he stayed in his clothes and boots. He listened to the sounds of Stockton's night life echoing down the alleys and wondered if the past would visit him while he slept.

Stryker woke to the sound of voices, two of them, belonging to young men, or boys, obviously very drunk. Slurry silly talk, and staggering footfalls evidenced their state of intoxication. He thought they might pass by until one of them bumped into the Conestoga.

"Hey what are these wagons doing here?"

"I feel sick," said the other one.

"Let's see what's inside."

"Leave it. I'm goin' on."

"Hold up. I'm gonna look."

"Fuck you. Headin' home 'fore I puke."

Stryker heard the second one's boots stomping irregular footfalls down the back street. The boy stopped to retch and stumbled on. Some distance away, he threw up again, and then Stryker couldn't hear him anymore.

The boy by the wagon must have been listening to his buddy too, and when his friend had moved out of earshot, he began muttering to himself. "Fuck you too. Fuck you, fuck you, fuck you." He steadied himself against the side of the wagon until coming around behind it. Stryker had left the tailgate down and the boy rested his forearms on the floorboards to lean in. Squinting hard, he must have had a hard time seeing anything in the dark interior. He fumbled in his pockets and finally withdrew a box of matches, which he promptly dropped.

"Aw, goddamnit." He steadied himself by holding on to the tailgate and stretched down to pick up the matchbox. Clasping the box in two hands, he rested both elbows on the floorboards again. He shook it vigorously, listening for matches. He spilled half of them before he got one out. It took three tries, but he eventually positioned it to strike and lit it on the first try.

The boot drove the match into the boy's mouth, knocking three front teeth down his throat. His head snapped backward, and recoiled forward, in time for the second blow to flatten his nose. He fell away from the tailgate and dropped to his knees, blood pouring from his mouth and nose. Struggling to his feet, he staggered off in the same direction of his friend.

Inside the Conestoga, Stryker rolled over to go back to sleep. Rather, he tried to go back to sleep. Leigh's bloodied and blackened face wouldn't leave him alone. He'd found her broken body lying on the field. Before she died, she'd looked up at him and said his name. Her blond hair was matted with mud and blood. Her eyelids dropped over the crystal blue eyes and closed for the last time. Even though another man had switched the firing coordinates, sending the shell out of the safety zone, he should have double checked the settings on the gun. He had not, and now his wife lay in a grave. Shit, he told himself, it's been fifteen years. He still questioned his decision to leave her on the ground after she died. At the time, he felt she was no more. The lifeless body on the ground could not have known if he stayed, carried her back, or left her lying there. But he did what a practical man does. To have done anything else would've been a useless emotional response. Those who criticized him for doing what he did could kiss his ass. He cursed his own brain for constantly remembering Leigh as he did on too many nights. Why couldn't his damn visions just recall her smiling face instead?

"Mister Stryker?" Someone called-a low measured greeting.

Stryker rose on an elbow and peeked under the canvas. A woman, he couldn't tell who.

"Go round back."

She came round to the tailgate, but still he didn't recognize her. The woman struggled mightily, and Stryker didn't offer to help. Grunting and cursing, she lost her balance three times before she gained enough momentum to get her upper torso inside. Gripping one of his boots with both hands, she got the rest of her body into the wagon. Gathering her dress above the knees, she crawled on all fours to his side. She felt for his arm and pulled it open. Then she lay down and scooted next to him.

"You smell fresh and clean after your bath."

He recognized her.

"Were you joking at dinner?" she asked.

"No."

"Not tonight though."

"No, not tonight."

Agnes curled an arm across his chest, stretched her neck, and kissed him lightly on the cheek. "Can you just hold me for a while?"

"Sure." Stryker pulled her tighter against him.

She left before daybreak.

"Trouble last night?" Hihn asked as he loaded the girl's trunks into the Conestoga.

Stryker adjusted the cinch on the roan. "No."

"Saw blood behind *der* wagon. Looks like someone or something did some bleeding." Hihn came out from behind the wagon and started walking toward the hotel's rear entrance. "I have to go back in and settle *die* charges."

Stryker dropped the stirrup, lifted a boot to it, and swung into the saddle. "I'll ride with you 'til we get out of town, then move on out ahead."

Rachel and Kahla climbed onto the buckboard without the usual grousing. A good night's sleep and breakfast served on linen table-cloths brightened their spirits. Renard whistled while he brought the mules around. He lined up his team and then Hihn's, a courtesy he hadn't extended to his brother before. He'd always just tended to his own team, letting Hans handle the other mules. When Hihn emerged from the hotel's back door, he stood on the top step, amused by the smiling girls and his whistling brother. He glanced ahead to Stryker who was resting his forearm on the saddle horn.

By mid-morning, any vestiges of joviality had vanished. Dust, rising temperatures, and bone jarring seat boards wore the good moods down, and replaced it with weighty resignation. Hihn and Renard drove the freight wagons behind the Conestoga, and they only talked to the mules–who failed to hold up their end of the conversation. Rachel and Kahla, seated together as usual in the lead wagon, had chatted incessantly for the first few miles, mostly about their day and night in Stockton. Eventually their talk ran dry as the dusty trail, and they rode in silence until Rachel remembered something she overheard between Hihn and Renard.

"Hihny said there was a dried blood on the ground behind our wagon this morning. He asked Stryker about it."

"Wha'd Stryker say?" Kahla asked.

"He didn't."

"He didn't know?"

"No, I mean he didn't answer. Just got on his horse and rode off," Rachel said.

"What's wrong with that man? He never said a word about what we did for him," Kahla said. After that, the girls kept ruminations on the matter to themselves.

At high noon when Hihn halted the wagons to rest and water the mules, Stryker kept his distance, figuring if he returned to the wagons, he'd get more questions. The afternoon brought them near Tracy, where they camped instead of attempting to find lodging in the small town. Stryker joined the Hihns for supper, but his stony silence dampened any conversation after the meal. He led the roan out of earshot from the wagons and bedded down.

CHAPTER TEN

The next morning, Hihn roused Renard and the girls before dawn. The delays had cost them. Hihn wanted to get past the long trail ride and begin cutting lumber in Felton. Livermore, another day's ride, would be the last settlement until San Jose where they'd load the wagons, livestock, and themselves, on a train. Although the distance to San Jose stretched out another 35 miles from Livermore, he reassured everyone that they had enough food and supplies to make it. They'd camp at night, making frequent stops for water, and then rest in San Jose before boarding the train for Felton.

"We are skirting Livermore 'cause I want to reach San Jose in three more days," Hihn shouted to his brother, bringing up another team of mules. "We *vill* send a telegram to Hank, let him know we are coming and to get *der* men ready. He *vill* have to get cut areas with trim spars and map winch routes for our donkey. Then, I think from San Jose, we take train in." Hihn pulled his team in front of the first freight wagon, harnessing them to the swingletrees and eveners. Once he made the final adjustments, he went to help Renard, who was having trouble with his mules. "You seen Stryker this morning? Hihn asked, snugging up a harness.

"Must've left early," Renard grumbled. The two men walked the last team up together.

They'd hitched the mules to the Conestoga by the time Stryker rode into camp. He downed a cup of black coffee, nodded a thanks to Rachel, and headed back out on the roan. He really didn't know why he wore such a surly mood. He had no particular gripe; none more than usual anyway. Although Renard had begun to grate on him, Hihn and the girls were tolerable. But for the time being, he wanted to keep away from them.

Stryker rode ahead of the wagons and didn't rejoin the Hihns until late in the evening, two hours after sundown. Rachel and Kahla moved as shadows inside the Conestoga, where two hanging lanterns illuminated their movement. Renard sat by the campfire reading while Hihn walked the mule line, inspecting them one last time for the night. Stryker filled his plate with stew from a pot hanging over the fire. The coffee pot on a flat rock still held two-and-a-half cups of the steaming brew. He ate and drank the coffee in silence. The Hihns recognized and respected his desire, or need, to keep his distance. Times in the past, he'd been forced to communicate, and those contacts did not bode well for man — or woman. With that in mind, he bedded down some distance away from camp. Perhaps tomorrow would be better.

The following day, the wagons swung south, skirting Livermore and wound their way up the Diablo Mountains. A light but steady rain had fallen most of the morning, soaking the treeless hills, the runoff making rivulets in the road. Coming from the east, the Diablos began with rambling, grassy foothills rising up after miles of relatively flat terrain. The wagons followed alongside railroad tracks which snaked through the hills; eventually reaching the thousand-foot Altamont Pass before dropping to a lower elevation and heading southwest.

Stryker rounded the last hill prior to the pass, which was actually two separate passes, the second one higher than the first. There, up ahead about a quarter mile, he saw an overturned coach. Ordinarily, the scene of a stagecoach mishap would not be suspicious, but Hihn's caution and the run-in with bandits caused Stryker to wheel the roan and ride back to the wagons. He'd seen people by the coach. However, they were too far away to know if they posed a threat. Whether they had caught sight of him, he couldn't tell.

"Got a stagecoach on its side 'round that hill." Stryker thumbed up the trail. "I'll ride with you."

"Anybody hurt?" Rachel asked.

"Don't know. Keep guns handy."

Rachel reached for the shotgun behind the seat. "Are you expecting trouble?"

"Make sure they're loaded and ready to fire," Stryker ordered. He pulled his own carbine and chambered a round. He didn't need to check the Peacemaker by his hip. It always stayed ready. After riding on back to the uncles' wagons, he gave the same instructions to them. Stryker wheeled about and trotted the roan ahead of the lead mules. He rode easily in the saddle but with the carbine resting in the crook of his arm, holding the reins, and with fingers circling the trigger guard.

Upon rounding the hill, the stagecoach came into view again. As Stryker got closer, it became clear there had been an accident. The coach, already dangerously tilted on the steep ground, had run its downhill wheels into a deep rut, deep enough to flip it on its side.

A man wearing a long duster broke away from the small crowd huddled by the overturned coach and came running toward Stryker, waving his arms. Getting closer, he slowed to a quick walk, breathing heavily and coughing.

"Hold your wagons, mister!" he yelled, angrily. "The road's bad. You'll have to go around." He stopped fifty paces in front of the roan and bent over, holding his knees and gasping. When he straightened and saw the Winchester pointed his way, he got less angry, "We got a lady hurt real awful. Y'all got a doctor or somebody who knows doctoring? She needs help."

"No doctor," Stryker answered.

"We'll look at her," Rachel said, setting the hand break. She climbed down from the Conestoga. "Bring the medicine chest, Kahla."

Hihn and Renard jumped from the freight wagons and came scurrying around the Conestoga to hear about the accident. Kahla handed the medical box to Renard, and Hihn helped her down from the wagon. She snatched the box from Renard and ran to catch up with Rachel.

"Stay vith *die* wagons, Renard." Hihn took off after his nieces, running past Stryker on the roan. Stryker rode behind the Hihns, who walked quickly to the overturned coach. He swung from the saddle and followed them as they approached the small crowd clustered around the injured woman. The group reluctantly parted for the girls, apparently not happy to relinquish front row views. Rachel and Kahla knelt on each side of the woman who lay motionless on the wet, grassy slope. Mud caked the front of the rose-colored dress and matted her hair where she had been pinned face down in the road. Someone had swiped her face, but splotches of the blackish mud still remained caked on her cheeks and forehead. Rachel opened the medical kit.

"She's banged up on the inside, back broke too, we think," one of the men volunteered. "Fell out when the coach rolled. Top rail pinned her. We got her out and laid her here, but she's passed out."

Rachel took charge. She carefully unbuttoned the woman's dress and loosened her bodice. Swelling in the lower abdomen indicated internal bleeding, and bluish welts around the ribs meant some were broken. Without professional medical help, it was clear the woman would not survive. Although Rachel could set bones and tend to surface wounds, she dared not cut into the woman's stomach and chest.

"I think all we can do is make her comfortable. If she comes to, I can give her pain medication, but even that may do more harm than good. I'm afraid the poor woman is not long for this world." Rachel folded the sides of the dress together. "Put a blanket on her to keep her warm."

In an uncharacteristic act, Stryker pulled down his bedroll and laid it over the victim, covering her up to the neck. The stricken woman opened her eyes and blinked several times to focus. She tilted her head slightly and saw the kneeling mixed-breed.

"You just never know, do you, Stryker?" Her eyelids floated together for the last time, and Agnes Kingsley departed this world.

Rachel placed an ear to her chest. "She's dead."

"If you men can help us bury her and right the coach, we'll get out of your way," the stage driver offered. "Get out too far off the road, you'll have trouble." He gave the warning as an enticement to help with the burial and righting the coach. The dead woman was now just an impediment to a man on a schedule.

"Well, let us get to it." Hihn said.

Stryker retrieved his bedroll and re-rolled it behind his saddle.

"You knew that woman?" Rachel asked incredulously, running up next to Stryker.

He picked up the reins and headed back to the wagons leading the roan.

Kahla, who suddenly broke into a sprint to catch the two, wanted to hear what Stryker had to say.

"Long enough to learn something," Stryker mumbled more to himself than anyone else.

"What's that?" Kahla asked, breathlessly.

"I'm too damn friendly."

Hihn brought the freight wagons forward, one on each side of the overturned stagecoach, and slung ropes over the wagons to the coach. Using the two mule teams pulling in opposite directions, they managed to lift the coach upright without damaging its wheels. They kept the uphill mules roped to the coach until it had been safely pulled out of the rutted section of the road. Once it rolled to flatter ground, they drew it off to the side and used handheld ropes to steady the Conestoga and freight wagons past the deep ruts. They buried Agnes in a shallow grave and marked it with a cross made from two spare wheel spokes.

CHAPTER ELEVEN

The cloud cover burned off not long after the Hihns left the stagecoach mishap and the Diablos became less challenging. Traveling farther southeast, the wagons dropped to gentler hills with plenty of watering holes. In another two days, the Hihns' outfit rolled into San Jose.

At mid-morning, they entered town from the northeast and continued down Market Street to the commercial center. They first stopped at the rail station where Hihn hired a crew of six men to pull the boiler, engine, and skid logs off the two freighters and assemble the steam donkey.

"We've got time to kill again," Kahla said to Rachel, watching the men work. The girls set off searching for a place to spend the night. They finally located a boarding house, a two-story residence, which had become the Rutledge Room and Board, after Mr. Rutledge died.

Renard directed the men assembling crankshafts, gears, brake handles, and then the smaller mechanical pieces. Afterward, he had them load the steam donkey on one of the freight wagons. Hihn and Stryker went to the ticket office, where Hihn made arrangements for five passengers and the freight shipment to Felton. The ticket-master told Renard which rail cars to load, and then Hihn asked him for directions to a store that sold oil and grease.

Off in the distance, a train whistle blew, then again shortly before the locomotive rounded a hill covered with berry bushes and chugged into view. On it came, slowing as it approached, drawing longer spaces between bellows of steam, with the engine rattling and clanging as if it were ready to crumble into a huge pile of metal. It gave one last dying gasp of steam as the train braked to a complete stop.

Later on, the crew rolled the freight wagon with the assembled steam donkey on it, across the platform and winched it up the loading ramp, and onto a flatcar.

"Did you measure height?" Hihn asked, walking onto the platform after being gone all afternoon. "Looks top heavy."

"Ain't no tunnels to Felton," Renard said.

"All the same, looks top heavy to me." Hihn scrunched his face. "Unload them."

"You sure Hans?" Renard asked.

"Unload them. Put *der* freighter and donkey on separate cars."

"Hans, how are we get'n that donkey off the wagon and on the flatcar?" Renard asked. "Our men can't lift that thing. And *you* said load 'em this way,"

"We didn't haul it all this way to lose it off *der* train, Renard. Roll it off. Then bring *der* wagon alongside *die* platform." Hihn shot a straight arm to point at a section of the platform nearest the rail car. "Break out jacks and tackle, then winch the donkey off *der* wagon and up ramp onto the flatcar. Tie it down good once you get it loaded. If we must, we can fire up steam donkey, but I believe that *vill* work."

"Untie and roll it off." Renard said to the crew. The men grumbled among themselves, purposely grousing loud enough for the brothers to hear.

Renard began to gripe with the crew as well until one of the older men, the kind of worker who knows a job must be done and does it, said, "C'mon let's do what the man says."

"Stryker, you help'n?" Renard saw him leaning against a corner of the station building, looking mildly interested.

"I am going to get myself a cup of coffee." Stryker shoved himself from the corner and headed up the street to find it.

Hihn took three men and loaded the Conestoga wagon. Once they'd rolled it on the flatcar, they used jacks to raise it and remove the wheels. They lowered the wagon bed onto a pair of rail ties bolted to the flatcar and lashed it down. "Good," Hihn said, wiping his forehead with a handkerchief. "Let us help Renard and *der* men and go to Felton."

Renard's workers had finished wrenching the steam donkey onto the rail car when Hihn and his men joined them. "We gotta tie it down and we'll be done." Renard puffed, slapping his hands together.

They used the remaining daylight and another two hours by lantern to complete the loading and freight tie-down. Renard, exhausted from the day's work and too tired to talk, dragged along beside Hihn, following Kahla and Stryker to the boarding house.

Rachel met them at the door. "Dinner's on the table, but it's cold. Follow me." The men filed behind her and down a narrow hallway, dark except midway where a flickering wall lantern danced shadows of silhouettes on faded brown wallpaper and a grandfather clock. When they entered the kitchen, Rachel swooshed flies away from a stained linen shroud before lifting it off a red checkered tablecloth, beneath which lay a small piece of meatloaf, a nearly empty bowl of mashed potatoes, and a two-day-old hunk of hardened baked bread.

"Sorry, we asked them to leave more. They, the other four men staying here, said they would, but this is all that's left," Rachel said apologetically. "Coffee's still warm." She turned their cups upright and filled them with lukewarm brew.

"I'm worn out," Renard said, after eating his meager portion. He lay his fork down and toyed with the coffee cup before slowly bringing it up for the final swallow.

"Me too," Hihn added, catching a contemptuous scowl from his brother.

"Another cup will do." And that summed up Stryker's dinner dialog, although he wasn't so quite worn out. He took ten minutes to finish the coffee and then left to go unfurl his bedroll down at the stables. He rightly assumed no offer to sleep at the boarding house was payback for his lack of loading help.

"I am going to bed too," Hihn said. He pushed back from the table.

⚔

Rising at dawn, Stryker saddled the roan and rode to the boarding house for breakfast. Climbing the steps, he read an ad written on the chalkboard by the door. He reasoned Hihn could damn well pay for his "Breakfast 25 Cents." He'd finished the eggs and sausage with biscuits and gravy, washed down by a cup of hot black coffee, when Hihn walked into the kitchen.

Hihn took a chair at the eight-person table opposite Stryker. "You and Renard got an early start."

"Haven't seen your brother," Stryker replied.

"Another man eat before us?" Hihn asked Mrs. Rutledge, placing a full plate in front of him.

"He's the first," she said, her eyes on Stryker. "And you owe twenty-five cents for 'im."

Hihn glanced at the impassive mixed-breed, then dug the money out from his pocket for Stryker's breakfast. He'd already paid for the others and, although two bits wasn't much, it annoyed him. He slapped the coin down. Mrs. Rutledge took it and briskly walked from the kitchen to her room, where she dropped it in her money jar.

"That train leaves at nine o'clock this morning. Renard better be there, but something tells me he is not. Stryker, I know you was not hired on for finding lost souls, but I would be obliged if you went looking for him," Hihn said cutting into a sausage.

Stryker allowed a perfunctory nod before getting to his feet. He lifted his gun belt off the wall peg where he'd hung it for breakfast and left to find Mrs. Rutledge.

She told him someone left the house earlier at two in the morning. "I'm certain of the time because I heard him moving about and thought it time to get up and cook breakfast, but when I come downstairs, the clock only chimed two times and weren't no one here."

Stryker walked out of the boarding house and, squinting, raked his eyes up and down the street before stepping down to undo the reins. He mounted up and pulled the roan away from the hitching rail. Keeping the big horse at a slow walk, he rode to the train depot and on to the mill. He went down each alley working his way back toward the boarding house and got the same answer when he questioned those he met.

"Looking for a man, medium build, forties, named Renard."

"No, ain't seen him."

Stryker returned, hitched the roan at the Rutledge House, and took long lanky strides to Chinatown, a few buildings clustered together to form the Asian enclave. He'd finally gotten a lead on Renard's whereabouts from a Chinaman standing by the boarding house steps. He hadn't seen the brother but said the only place a man would go in the middle of night was Kwong Hong On's, an opium den whose entrance was gained through a cluttered alley two streets over.

At the passageway's end, the two-story building stood alone. Three wide, black steps led to a large red door adorned with a green carved dragon above the entrance. Smaller dragons hung at the lower corners, and a red overhang ran along the second story roofline. There was enough room for a person to pass between it and the buildings on each side, thus allowing visitors to approach from the front and enter through the back door.

Stryker climbed the steps, swung the brass handle on the red door, and entered the opium den. A second red door appeared in the vestibule situated so that it opened after the outside door closed, blocking sunlight from entering the den. He had to ring a bell and wait for the second door to unlock. When it opened, the foul-smelling vapors, like those of a rotting carcass, invaded his nostrils. He saw a small desk with a smudged oil lamp casting flickering illumination on cadaverous souls lying on matted bunks. They lay there in a drugged stupor, staring out from their beds with vacant eyes. A Chinaman approached from the shadows carrying a bowl and a pipe, complete with an opium pill stuck at the end of a bamboo stem.

Stryker shoved the offering into the Asian's chest. "Looking for a white man, need light to find him."

"We keep room dim, for relaxation. Windows painted black. You want candle?" The Chinaman spoke with lacquered graciousness.

Stryker pointed to a black rectangle two paces to his left, "That a glass window?"

The Asian bowed deeply. "It is."

Stryker spun and smashed a straight-armed hammer fist to the bowing Chinaman's left temple. The blow knocked the stunned man a quarter turn, facing him toward the window. Stryker gripped his Tang jacket collar and the seat of the man's pants with his other hand. He ran the Chinaman across the floor and *opened* the window. Though sunlight flooded the den, hardly any of the occupants noticed. Another window was set far back on the opposite wall and he opened it with his boot. Quick inspection of the bunks didn't turn up Renard. The one white man, who looked to be in his late teens, lay motionless on the floor.

"Help." A girl sobbed.

Stryker heard the cry coming from behind a bunk pushed away from the wall. He stepped around it and found a white girl, nearly naked, her blue dress crumpled around her armpits. The girl's wrists, bruised and swollen, were lashed to two iron rings bolted to the wall. Her legs were splayed spread-eagled, secured at the knees with leather straps buckled to other bolts in the floor. A red silk pillow positioned under the belly raised her hips, allowing for easy access from behind.

"Help me, please."

"Not your lucky day, Miss," Stryker said, turning away to look for Renard.

"My boyfriend brought me here to smoke and I don't know what happened to him. These pigs tied me up like this. I don't know how many have raped me."

"How long you been here?"

"Days, I guess. Does it matter? Please."

"Any other white men been here besides that boy over there?"

"Yes. He left."

"He have a German accent?"

"I think so."

"You see him?"

"I can't see shit, dammit!" She jerked against the restraints. "I hurt down there. My butt's bleeding. Half of 'em used the wrong hole. For God's sake! I'll pay you!"

"I don't see any pockets."

"My father's got money. I'll pay one hundred dollars."

"Reckon, he's got lots of daughters," Stryker said, surveying the room in between glances at the door.

"A thousand!"

Stryker fished the straight razor from his pocket. She got to her feet remarkably quick, although she had to steady herself against him, and when she started to walk, her numbed feet couldn't keep her balanced. She turned away, yanked the dress down past her hips, and faced him again. The girl was nearly a foot shorter than Stryker and thin, her hair blond, her face nicely cut, and her jawline defiant. "You'll have to carry me. Wait—another thousand to burn this place to the ground."

"Deal." Stryker flipped her arms up, knelt, and threw her over his left shoulder.

She felt his strong arm pin her legs to his chest, and she rested the side of her face, upside down, against his back. The boyfriend still lay on the floor. She started to call out and stopped. She stared at the body a moment longer and then closed her eyes. "Burn it."

As they made for the front, two men burst through the door, a large, muscular Asian armed with a bo staff, followed by the man who had *opened* the window, shards of glass were still stuck his forehead.

Stryker pulled the .44 and fired a round into the big Asian's chest. The second slug blew the smaller man out the door. Stryker smashed the gun barrel against the lamp, splashing oil onto a pile of straw mats. He rushed out the front doors, gun drawn.

He drooped the girl over the roan's neck, figuring she had a sore ass, and he climbed up behind her. "All right sweet cheeks, where's the two-grand?"

She flung out an arm. "Go down that street. Big yellow house at the end." Then she dropped her arm and braced both forearms against the roan's withers. "Let's go, I don't like being upside down," she groaned.

Ten minutes later they came to her home. The street turned into a road and the large yellow house rested at its end, a half mile from downtown San Jose. Stryker dismounted, placed his hands under the girl's hips, and slid her off, cradling her in his arms.

"Let me walk."

She grasped the handrail, climbed unsteadily up three spacious steps, and opened one of the tall, white doors. Stryker trailed inside.

"Father?" The girl's shout rang hollow in the big house. She straightened her dress. "Father!" Louder, but no answer. She led Stryker into the mahogany paneled parlor. She perched herself on the corner of a redwood desk, polished to a brilliant shine, and dangled her foot down to the plush carpet while they waited. A few minutes passed before she stood and faced him, and he noticed for the first time how blue her eyes were. She drew back and went around him. She walked from the parlor, limping badly. "He's ... he's not home," she said without looking back. "His horse and buggy would be out front." She crossed the entryway and steadied herself, gripping both hands on the staircase banister. "Mother . . .?" She called up the stairs. Turning around, she saw Stryker walking out of the parlor, "I wonder where everyone is."

"Your piggy bank better have . . ."

"Someone's coming." She rushed past Stryker and threw the door open, banging it against the wall. "Papo!"

Stryker noted she moved without obvious pain. He started to comment about it but figured two thousand dollars just rode up.

"Gloria! We've been looking all over for you. Where on earth have you been?" A man, likely in his early forties, in a well-cut brown suit, clean shiny boots, and a derby hat, bolted up the steps to hug his daughter.

"Your mother and I have been sick with worry. She's still looking for you now. Oh, honey!" He squeezed his daughter even tighter.

Stryker let the girl do all the talking. She told her father about a kidnapping and the plan to collect a ransom, leaving out the part about the opium den. Easy to do since the charred bodies in the den weren't talking. That Stryker had heard her cries for help in some unknown building (burned to the ground) in Chinatown and had gallantly charged in to save her. The kidnappers had wanted twenty-thousand, and she had promised her rescuer two.

"Two thousand dollars! That's a lot of . . .!"

"To rescue me, he shot two men." Gloria pushed gently back from her father.

His voice dropped a lot lower, ". . . money."

"Dead." Gloria dead-panned. The last came not as information, but as a warning.

"Thank you, sir. Thank you." Her father grabbed Stryker's hand and shook it.

The father turned to his daughter. "Did that boy have anything . . .?"

"Well . . ."

"I knew it." Her father raised a palm at his daughter. "Say no more. I told your mother and I've told you-many times-he's no good. Someday, some sad day, things would come to a bad ending cause o' that boy. I forbid you. I absolutely forbid you to ever see him again."

"I won't, Papo. Never again."

The grateful father paid the money without further complaint. He shook Stryker's hand vigorously a second time, thanking him for saving his only daughter from kidnappers and the fire. Although . . . if he'd been told the full story, the father would have probably torched Chinatown himself.

Twenty minutes later, Stryker met Hihn and the girls at the train depot, two-thousand dollars in his saddlebag.

Thirty minutes prior to the train leaving, Renard showed up. He offered no explanation as to his whereabouts, and Hihn, although irritated, didn't ask. The belching steam engine didn't accommodate easy conversation, anyway.

Stryker put the roan with the mules in the boxcar and the switchman pulled the lever, backing the train onto the side rail. The freight cars connected with a jolt and the rest of the travelers climbed aboard the two passenger cars. Workers loaded the stock cars behind the coaches, then the freight cars between the tinder and passenger cars. The coaches, unlike the Pullman's Palace coaches, lacked any hint of luxury. The interior had two rows of hard wooden seats with backs, plank floors, windows which partially opened only from the top down, and small vents in the curved roof. Kahla and Rachel sat opposite Hihn and Renard in one of the few seats facing rearward. Stryker sat across the aisle beside a priest with two nuns seated behind them. He pulled his hat brim down, folded his arms, and stretched out his long legs.

"Looks like a huge fire," Kahla leaned closer to the window. Beyond the immediate buildings to the north, huge plumes of gray smoke billowed skyward. Rachel crouched near her sister and craned her neck to look.

"Some fool started a fire in Chinatown," Renard said. "Gonna burn the whole town down. White folk just standing and watching it burn."

Stryker dropped the hat brim over his eyes and crossed his legs.

Later that same night, as Gloria eased her aching body into a claw-foot bathtub filled with warm, soothing water of bath salts and fragrances and thought about how painful a bad ending could be.

CHAPTER TWELVE

T he steam engine strained to pick up speed as it pulled out of San Jose. Several of the curious passengers scurried to the east side of the train car, to watch the flames of the fire shooting skyward. Hotels, stores, churches, and saloons, facing away from the fearsome inferno consuming Chinatown, were unaware of the flames marching toward them.

"Why don't they try to put it out?" A plump woman, with two children clinging to her dress, asked.

"Chinese can put out the fire," replied Renard, aggravated, the mother chose him to lean over for a view.

The priest decided not to drag his cassock over Stryker's outstretched legs and remained seated. Yet he sensed the tall man next to him wasn't snoozing, but simply ignoring the excitement. "These matters are of no interest to you?"

"No." Stryker answered under his hat.

"Those suffering, of no concern?" The priest pressed. He glanced rearward and tossed a smile at the nuns. They politely returned it, dipping their white cornetts.

"If God wanted the fire out, he'd make it rain," Stryker grunted.

"An interesting philosophical concept you have broached, my

friend. You suggest God's work be more obvious, more direct, instead of through human means."

"Me and God leave each other alone. You should follow his lead." Stryker tipped the brim back with a long tan finger and squinted a warning toward the holy man.

"So, the metaphysical is . . .?" The priest began, paying no heed to the warning.

"Outside the world. Ride that trail later," Stryker interrupted.

Now the curiosity of the priest was piqued. He cocked an eyebrow at the nuns who bowed their heads again and tried a different tactic. "Some religions say seventy-two virgins may await you." He offered a nascent grin.

"Keep the virgins. Gimme the whores. They know how to please a man."

What Stryker knew, he knew clearly. What was unknowable, he ignored. Those who challenged him either physically or verbally valued their lives cheaply. A man whose sole objective in life is to remain alive, savagely fighting for survival, is a dangerous man. But even though he fought fiercely, he did not fear death. He believed someday another man would end his life. He would not grow old. His only belief, if called that, was that he existed and one day would not.

The priest got off easily. He only got Stryker's pragmatism.

The train chugged along and San Jose with its fire faded out of sight. Folks returned to their wooden seats and conversations migrated on to other topics. Forested foothills loomed directly ahead of the lumbering train, waiting to challenge the Shay steam engine. The narrow-gauge track began curving up the grade, and the additional workload slowed its speed.

The conductor, a short, portly fellow with a bushy, tobacco-stained mustache, entered the car and began punching tickets. He said "ticket" as a greeting to each traveler. Those who held out their tickets without prompting got nothing. Hihn held all the purchased tickets and presented them for validation. The conductor took them, fanned the five out and cocked his eyebrows at Hihn.

"Me, *die* two girls, him and him," Hihn said, pointing first at his nieces, and then Renard and Stryker.

The conductor clicked the single-hole puncher five times, gave the tickets back to Hihn, and moved to the next aisle.

"Friendly fellow," Hihn said to himself, but loud enough for the conductor, who disregarded the comment.

The rhythmic rocking motion sent Kahla toward slumber. Her head canting ever so slowly, came to rest on Rachel's shoulder. Rachel dozed too, struggling mightily to remain upright and trying not to disturb Kahla. Hihn daydreamed, gazing out the window at the changing landscape, passing by more slowly as the train lumbered uphill. Renard snored.

Stryker couldn't sleep, but he did relax with his outstretched legs under the forward bench. For the first time since he left Egalitaria, his thoughts drifted back to the woman he had known, albeit only for a few days . . . Morgan Bickford, a hard-assed, strong-willed woman, who had a philosophical penchant for individual freedom, and who'd fought for it. He remembered how she looked when speaking in front of a crowd the night they shot her, straight and proud. Stryker had given politics little thought until he met Morgan, a woman alone, waging war against a Marxist gang of murderous thugs.

Morgan had persuaded him to fight the gang alongside her, and he'd managed to kill off most of them, but not before she took a bullet. Her son reported the news of her death to him . . . and the kid got a busted nose for it.

Many years had passed since Stryker's wife died. He'd assuaged his natural urges with women who simply wanted a man, any man. The dark hours sitting across from midnight can be lonely. And sure, some wanted a few dollars. Morgan, though, was different–way different. She elicited a passion within him which far exceeded lust in the loins. He had not felt such passion since Leigh, and even then, it had not been with the fire Morgan kindled. Her passion for her principles was infectious, and when combined with physical attractiveness, they threatened his memories of Leigh. He cleared his throat.

Stryker had allowed himself to eventually respond to Morgan, knowing all other ventures of emotion ended violently, tragically. This one had too. Now the man some called Evil would live much like a snarling wounded animal, reacting to aggression with a gun and a blade, leaving most foes dead.

The conductor, still punching tickets, shuffled past Stryker to the rear of the car. A schoolteacher sitting in a row ahead turned as if to summon the conductor, but she gazed at Stryker instead. He lifted his face and the woman saw two slivers of pale gray eyes staring back. His week-old beard cracked open and his lips curled back. The woman turned forward and picked up a book and then laid it on her lap.

The terrain, now thick with black and coast oak, maple, Douglas fir, and a spattering of other trees, steepened. The train crawled laboriously up the narrow-gauge track. Each time they rounded a curve, Stryker could see the Shay locomotive working hard, blowing powerful puffs of steam, with the tender car behind it and another coach car between the tender and his car. At times, the rails cut through hills where banks along the tracks became walls and one could reach out to touch them. Then the walls would suddenly drop away, and they'd cross trestles built high upon bents and braces, bridging gulches or valleys.

Stryker sensed something wrong when he heard the hissing bellows slow their cadence. The decelerating train finally came to a complete stop. Up ahead and out of sight, the engine continued to puff away, albeit with lengthy pauses between each release. The coach car had come to rest with twenty-foot cliffs on each side, so that the windows only offered views of earthen walls. Hihn pivoted to make eye contact with Stryker, who had already gotten to his feet with the .44 in hand.

Three middle-aged women traveling together, who could have been sisters, sat behind the Hihn brothers. The one nearest the aisle saw the gun first. "In heaven's name we ask!" For some reason, she uttered a mealtime blessing to alert the other two. Scrunching together, clutching their purses, the three sought safety from each other, evidently thinking the mixed-breed a train robber. The nearby men shifted uncomfortably; seemingly pressed to act, and yet hesitant to challenge the man with a drawn gun.

"Everyone stay calm. Mister Stryker, would you please see why we have stopped?" Hihn asked. His request elicited murmurs of relief, except for the three women who remained huddled together.

Stryker turned and opened the door to the rear platform. He stepped outside and leaned over the safety railings on both sides to inspect the train, front and rear, but it had stopped on a curve and the steep walls limited his vision. He swung back into the coach and took quick strides toward the front. By that time, other men had left their seats and Stryker shoved them out of the way, some onto the laps of those still seated. However, protestations were directed at the train stoppage and prudently, not at the tall man with the drawn Colt.

The conductor opened the wood-paneled door and burst inside, coming to an abrupt halt with the barrel of the .44 inches from his chest.

"Why'd we stop?" Stryker demanded.

The railroader raised his hands and stepped back. "Folks, there's been a delay. The trestle is out ahead of us." He dropped his hands when Stryker holstered the gun. Breathing easier, he continued. "We think we can repair it, but it'll take a few hours."

"What's the damage?" one of the men asked.

"A rail's come loose and fallen down the gorge. We have to . . ."

"You need help?" Another asked before the conductor could finish.

"The gorge is deep and steep. Ain't gonna be easy getting it up. And yeah, we could use all the help we can get. Volunteers follow me."

Something in the conductor's eyes, lingering on every male, seemingly dealing each an accusatory card for a reaction, told Stryker there might be more to the loose rail story. "What kind of help?" He asked.

"Sure-footed men with strong backs," the conductor replied. Then he returned his attention to Stryker. "Don't know of a need for firearms, not yet anyway. What's your business, mister?"

"Mister Stryker's with us, sir," Hihn interjected. "My brother and me *vill* be glad to be of assistance," he said, rising to his feet. "Come, Renard."

Renard got to the aisle and followed his brother. Brushing past Stryker, he asked, "Care to join us?"

Stryker didn't immediately follow.

The Hihn brothers and the conductor had already stepped off the train before he made up his mind. He had no intention of helping, but the rail man had more information to give. Four other men, two stout and two more who thought they were, rose and shuffled forward.

Outside, the group of eight walked single file past the first passenger car where three more men joined them. The new work party marched by the engine, puffing the last vestiges of steam against their trouser legs.

Up ahead of the resting locomotive, the earthen walls fell away, and the rails stretched across a trestle bridging a forty-foot chasm. The men climbed between the tracks and walked the rail ties until they came to the missing rail, one third across the trestle. A single spike remained on a tie; the rest had fallen with the rail. They could see it, barely visible in the heavy brush below.

"That rail come loose somehow, ended up down there. It's damn steep and it ain't gonna be easy haulin that thing up here. Sorry, don't have no rope. We gotta carry it." The conductor sought confirmation from the brakeman who had just joined them on the trestle. "You got any other ideas, George?"

"That 'bout sizes it up." George agreed.

"I got a jenny can pull that rail. Need cable to it," Hihn offered.

"Ain't a mule alive that can pull that rail up here, even if it got down there in one piece," George said, chuckling amid guffaws from some of the men. What we need is a strong rope and mules. Mules we got."

"Once we get cable on it, my steam donkey *vill* bring it up." Hihn said, sounding confident.

The conductor hesitated, sizing up the German. "All right. Well, looks like the base plates are still on it. A loop on one of them should hold. I don't reckon any other trains are due, but we better send a man up the track and one down, til we're movin' again," George said, acknowledging Hihn's plan.

While they debated the plan, Stryker knelt by the missing rail section, inspecting the ties. Running his fingers over crowbar indentations, he determined the rail had been intentionally removed and wondered why the rail men hadn't said as much. He rose and stepping two ties at a time, made his way to the flat car carrying the steam donkey. It sat securely aboard the car and didn't appear tampered with; nevertheless, Stryker continued down the train, found the roan and returned with the .44-40 carbine.

Gripping a handrail to the flat car holding the steam donkey, he swung himself onto it. He settled down between its wooden skids and propped his back against the boiler with the carbine across his lap.

"Well, Mister Stryker. I see you have fondness for my little jenny," Hihn said upon finding his hired gunman guarding the logging machine.

Lady luck had helped load the donkey. The winches faced toward the engine, allowing the cable to spool toward the trestle. The German organized a bucket brigade from the stream that fed the gorge, filled the boiler, and then fired it up. Renard managed to fashion a makeshift ramp with two planks he found on another freight wagon and brought up a mule to haul the cable. The bucket crew found an old game trail where the tracks cut through the hill, and they scrambled up it to sit on the bank to watch. The steam donkey's belching and clanging sounded like a smaller version of the Class B 28-ton Shay locomotive.

Hihn smiled to himself, knowing why the men sat high on the banks to be out of harm's way in case the boiler blew, or the cable snapped, or to just have a good view of things. Renard and one of the stout passengers walked the mule, pulling the cable along the track and out onto the trestle. They unbuckled the hook and cable off the mule and let it fall. Once men below attached it to the rail, Renard signaled the brakeman who circled a raised an arm for Hihn to start the winch. Hihn opened the throttle and pulled the friction jam back, allowing the haul back drum to rewind the cable. He couldn't resist giving two sharp blasts on the whistle.

Stryker had to acknowledge he admired, maybe even liked the damn German, working his machine.

Stryker moved to the forward platform of the coach car, but the steep embankments limited his vision and the puffing engines hampered hearing. Holding the carbine in a firing grip with one hand, he climbed the iron ladder to the roof, two rungs at a time, crawled to the front edge, and lay down in a prone position. Even though he was now level with both banks, thick trees and brush impeded his view. Hihn, on the donkey, made a limited target because of the car ahead and the banks, but Stryker figured a concealed rifleman could still have a shot at him. Scanning ahead, smoke and steam partially obscured the trestle and beyond it, but not enough to completely shield two mounted horses and a rider-less third horse, drop out of the trees a quarter mile up the tracks.

The cable snapped taut as the engine chugged away, its pistons driving in rhythmic cadence. Abruptly the skids canted right, the crankshaft strained to rotate the drum, and it seemed as if the steam donkey would pull itself off the flatcar. Then the rail in the gulch broke through a tree root and the steel projectile flew up and out of the gulley, landing by the brakeman smoking a cigarette.

The startled brakeman almost swallowed his smoke. He danced a jig as the rail plowed by his dancing boots, and he kept dancing even after the rail skidded by him.

"Kill the engine!" Renard yelled, running past the startled brakeman who finally stopped dancing, to begin his best cussing.

Men on the banks erupted with loud guffaws, slapping their thighs. The close call followed with the brakeman's dance turned the potential tragedy into a comedy. Hihn pushed the gear lever halfway forward, throwing the winch out of gear, and then full forward, reversing it to slacken the cable. Renard tried loosening the cable on the rail, but the difficult yank had tightened the loop, partially buried in mud, and he couldn't work it free.

"You laughing hyenas, get down here and get this rail up. God damn it all! Grab the carry tongs!" the brakeman roared. He approached the rail as if it would attack him again and bent down to inspect it. "We gotta slide the goddamn thing back and lift it out. Shit fire!"

The men sitting on the bank continued to laugh and mimic the dancing brakeman by leaning back and jiggling their legs.

"Get down here, damnit!"

Still laughing, they goaded each other off the embankment. The engineer handed them tongs and showed them how to grip the rail.

"Okay now, slide it out. Knock the cable off with a hammer or rock. Get on each side, and walk it out there," the brakeman ordered. "We ain't got all day." The work went smoothly. They pounded spikes back into the same holes. It would have gone quicker if some of the men didn't stop to dance jigs.

Stryker squinted over the Winchester, shifting the gun barrel from left to right and back again, searching section by section. Occasionally he glanced to the rear, though he figured a man with a rifle would most likely be ahead, sighting on Hihn or Renard. The steam donkey's racket drowned out everything else, and it made him uneasy. A shot wouldn't sound out, so he had to rely on what he could see. The German kept the steam donkey running, evidently enjoying, for him anyway, the melody of the driving pistons. He stood on a skid with spread legs, hands on hips.

Stryker let his eyes linger momentarily on Hihn, admiring the German and his machine. Gradually, his focus adjusted, moving from the prideful figure to the boiler where a small wisp of vapor escaped from its side wall about chest high. Suddenly it clicked in his mind. The vapor wasn't there before. It blew from a small hole . . . a bullet hole.

Stryker yelled a warning. No good. Hihn faced away from him. He couldn't see Stryker motion to him either. Stryker steadied the carbine on the roof's edge, taking aim at less than fifteen feet. The bullet drilled through Hihn's hat, creasing his scalp, and ricocheting off a coupler to lodge itself in a bystander's gun belt. The force of the bullet spun the man around, causing him to lose balance, and he fell, smashing his face against a rail tie.

Hihn dove for cover between the skids. He looked up and saw Stryker on top of the coach car.

"Stryker!"

"Stay down! Kill it!" Stryker pointed at the steam donkey and ran a forefinger across his throat.

Hihn couldn't hear him, but he understood the signal. Stretching his arm over the skid rail, he hit the throttle valve, closing it. The donkey engine coughed twice and then died. "Stryker!"

"Stay down, damnit!" Stryker ordered.

Another shot sent wood chips flying off a skid's top edge. But this time Stryker heard it. He sent three rounds in rapid succession toward a clump of white pines on the far side of the gulch, quickly working the lever three times, then a slow fourth while looking for movement. A figure wearing a red shirt flashed on the other side of the gully and then disappeared into a thick cover of green boughs. He placed two more slugs slightly higher up the hill and waited.

The rail men and volunteers leapt from the tracks and flattened themselves against the dirt banks. Several quiet minutes slipped by after Stryker's last two shots before one of the men called up to him. "Hey mister, y'all done shootin'?" They got no answer, and one by one the men cautiously got to their feet. Stryker remained lying on the roof, slowly working the gun barrel back and forth, searching for the shooter.

Hihn rose and felt his scalp before replacing his hat. "Renard, come look," he said, as he inspected the bullet hole still releasing steam.

Renard climbed over a skid to reach Hihn and although Stryker couldn't hear them, he reckoned they discussed the boiler's repair.

Eventually, everyone climbed aboard the coaches and the Shay engine began belching powerful bursts of steam. Just before the straining locomotive pulled the couplings tight, Stryker climbed off the roof and trotted to the passenger car. He hopped aboard, opened the rear door, and stepped inside. The mounting rattle of turning wheels flooded in behind Stryker as the passengers turned to see who'd entered. Stryker shut the door and all, except the priest, Hihn, and his nieces went back to what they were doing. Hihn evidently decided not to broach the subject of the shooting in front of the others, and the girls merely watched Stryker retake the bench next to the cleric. The priest engaged the mixed-breed in a new round of conversation when the conductor interrupted.

"We should arrive at the Felton station within an hour barring no further problems."

The conductor walked front to back, stooping to peer out the windows as he made his way rearward. He stopped at the door and looked behind as if to insure no one followed him before he opened it. Standing on the rear platform, he dug out cigarette makings, curled the paper with a forefinger and poured a line of tobacco on it. The train chugged slowly up the grade, straining to pick up speed from a full stop. The rail man put the tobacco pouch in his coat pocket before rolling the cigarette and sealing it with a lick. He struck a match and cupped his hands to light the smoke. He took a deep drag.

The man in the red plaid shirt stepped out from behind a redwood's broad trunk and easily kept pace with the laboring train. He grabbed a handrail and hauled himself onto the platform next to the conductor.

"Good shootin' Al," the conductor said sarcastically. He inhaled again and blew smoke out in a huff.

"Yeah, I know, Carter. But the only time he stood alone wuz by that machine and you stopped too soon. Angle was no good. You could've pulled the train up more."

"George tried to get the engineer to pull up, but he said he'd need room to run flat 'fore we hit the grade. An', don't go in there with the rifle." The conductor pointed at Al's gun with the cigarette.

"Ain't leavin' it."

"Hop off and get in the last car then." The conductor took one last drag and flipped the stub at the coupling. "I gotta piss." He dropped the uniform trousers, poked his penis through his long johns, and sent a stream arcing forty feet off another trestle, to the gulch below.

"Bet five dollars I can beat-cha," Al challenged, fumbling with his pants.

Neither man noticed Stryker, who'd stepped outside to empty his own bladder.

Carter strained to stretch his stream. "Heyman's gonna be pissed too. We didn't get the German. Ah . . ., can't push no more." His arc drooped.

"You owe me five dollars," Al bragged. "An' I'll plug him 'fore we see Heyman."

Stryker placed one hand on the platform rail and gripped the car ladder with the other. Supporting himself by his arms, he leaned backward and swung his feet up. He jammed his boots into their backs and shoved.

"Whoa . . . shit!" Carter cried.

Al bellowed, "Ah . . . fuck!"

Their arms flailed windmills and legs pedaled invisible bicycles–as much as they could with their pants around their knees until they painted a vivid portrait of their deaths on a large flat rock below.

Seeing the men paste themselves on the rock caused a corner of Stryker's mouth to twitch. He undid his trousers and launched his own stream. It reminded him this Heyman man was beginning to piss him off.

When Stryker seated himself back in the coach, the priest asked, "Everything okay?"

"Yeah."

The train chugged into Felton ninety minutes later.

"Hey, is this Felton?" Kahla asked her uncle.

"This is it." Hihn answered, loud enough for all in the coach to hear.

"Odd the conductor didn't come by to make the announcement," the priest whispered to Stryker.

"He got off the train with another man." Stryker stood and stretched.

CHAPTER THIRTEEN

Felton's population numbered around three hundred, give or take a few itinerant Chinese laborers who made up one-fourth of the town's inhabitants. The narrow-gauge rails being laid up the San Lorenzo Valley had yet to reach Boulder Creek, and the loggers still operated flumes down to Felton. From there, the Santa Cruz and Felton Railroad hauled lumber to the Santa Cruz wharf. Felton, a bustling logging town, had become the valley's main junction for receiving, milling, and shipping logs. The flume terminus that fed logs to the sawmill sat east of the tracks opposite the depot building, and near to the San Lorenzo River. Felton's commercial and residential buildings, mostly unpainted, spread west of the depot. A few trees stood uncut in the valley floor; however, the slopes lay stripped up to the ridgelines on both sides of the town.

Hank Ledbetter, Hihn's crew foreman, met the train with a flatbed wagon specially built to haul the steam donkey. The narrow-gauge railroad actually extended up to Pacific Mills, Hihn's company headquarters, but Hank had fabricated the wagon in Felton, and Hihn decided to carry the donkey the last three miles on it. He pulled the wagon alongside a temporary platform constructed a hundred feet or so south of the depot. The train engineer backed the rail car next to the platform, and

Hihn used the donkey to winch itself on the wagon. Renard put up a line rope around four trees by the river and two of Hank's men helped him move the mules and Stryker's roan to the makeshift corral.

"Had trouble. Someone shot at me," Hihn told Ledbetter, pull-testing the last half-hitch he'd set on the tie-down.

"What's that you say?" Hank shouted.

"What you hear in town?" Hihn yelled back. Sibilant steam releases from the locomotive and piercing wails from the big saw at the mill forced the shouting.

"Crews here in Felton talking 'bout forming a union. Same up in Pacific Mills, Boulder Creek, and all over the San Lorenzo valley. That rail strike's give 'em ideas." The saw stopped, and Hank lowered his voice. "And on top of that, we gotta cut deeper an' higher. Every outfit's lost men and ox pullin' 'em logs down these hills."

"Any *die* men in this 'union' talk?" Hihn stopped pulling on the rope.

"Feron asked me, what a union was. I told him a bunch of boys getting together to lose their jobs. He ain't asked me no more."

"You bring a team to haul that wagon?" Hihn nodded at the steam donkey on the flatbed. "Our mules gotta pull my wagons."

"Brung eight oxen." Hank answered. "Hans, before we head up to Pacific Mills, we gotta get logging rights higher up. While you been gone, most trees got cut up to the ridges, both sides of the valley, 'tween here and Pacific Mills. We either have 'ta go farther north or pay top dollar buying out some permits."

"What about other side over the ridges, Ben Lomond's *vest* ridge? It been cut?" Hihn asked.

"No, never bothered. Ox ain't pullin' logs uphill. Hard 'nough skidding 'em down. They got a flume now, down here to Felton from up past Pacific Mills and a new rail line coming farther up than that." Hank watched Rachel and Kahla get off the train. "Take logs all the way to Santa Cruz," he said, watching the girls turn and come his way. "And, and . . . Good Lord!" Struggling mightily, he tore his eyes from the eye-catching fräuleins and back to Hihn. "I mean, still them big redwoods are a lotta work gettin' to flume or rail."

If Hihn noticed his nieces distracted Hank, he didn't show it. "Hank, you fell white pines far side Ben Lomond, this donkey *vill* bring them up. Then we can skid down to the flume, or rail. Log permits that side *vill* be cheaper than the valley. Let the others cut redwoods. Them whites not so big. Where do I file?"

"Office on Cooper Street over there." Hank hooked a thumb over his shoulder. "No redwoods?"

"Told you this place stinks," Kahla said, walking up behind Hihn with Rachel and Stryker. Two porters carrying the girl's baggage trailed behind them. Stryker, beside the porters, rested the barrel of the Winchester on his shoulder.

"Hank, my two nieces, Rachel and Kahla." Hihn directed an upward palm at the girls. "*Der* friendly looking fellow *vith* them is Mister Stryker. He helped on our way here. This is Hank Ledbetter, my foreman." Hihn cut the introductions short and got back to business. "Redwood is too soft an' too big. Anyway, don't seem right, cutting those giant trees."

"The mill throws off piles of sawdust. It starts stinking when it rots," Hank explained to Kahla, attempting to light a spark.

"Suppose it is too late today. I *vill* visit the office in the morning. That a hotel?" Hihn pointed toward a two-story building with a vertical sign attached to the corner, its sign facing away from them.

"Yeah, the Cunningham House, only good one here." Hank said, nodding his head at the hotel. "Up Baldwin there, Felton's main street. Town's growing, though. Soon there'll be more hotels, saloons, churches, schools, libraries, and whorehouses-just like any other good town," Hank boasted, before his voice trailed off, realizing prostitution talk wouldn't be appropriate for the girls. He went awkwardly and spoke with far less enthusiasm. "Glad to make your acquaintances," Hank said, looking sheepish. He tipped his hat to the girls and threw a head nod to Stryker. Beating a retreat to the other side of the wagon, he began tugging on the tie-down ropes and cursing himself under his breath. "You dumb ass."

"Stryker," Hihn turned to the mixed-breed, who still shouldered the carbine. "You are a fair man. I only owe you for days you rode guard.

That time you missed 'cause of *der* bear was not a fault of mine. I subtracted hotel charges in Sacramento too, so I think you *vill* find this to be the correct amount." He handed an envelope to Stryker. "However, you can earn a bonus if you would stay longer. That is, if you would make your services available should I need you."

"I'll be heading north."

"North?" Kahla asked.

"San Francisco."

"Train?" Hank brushed his cap a little higher on his brow and rested both arms atop the wagon.

"Horse. There a trail?"

"Well, you could go along the San Lorenzo River to its headwater past Boulder Creek and then go a day's ride straight north to the Saratoga Trail. Follow it to the Big Basin Way Trail down to Saratoga. All told from here it's a two-day ride, three if you ain't in a hurry. Pacific Mills is three miles north, Boulder Creek seven miles farther." Hank pointed a forefinger. "Take that road."

Stryker stuffed the envelope inside his shirt and dropped the carbine off his shoulder. Holding the carbine next to the Peacemaker, he made for the makeshift corral. He ducked under the rope, pushed his way through the mules, and untied the roan. After opening the rope gate and leading the horse out, he re-tied the gate and mounted up. He rode about a hundred paces and crossed the tracks, settling on the road north.

"That's it? No goodbye, no got to go, no nothing?" Kahla whispered to Rachel.

"Ain't exactly verbose, your Mister Stryker." Hank allowed to no one in particular.

"No . . . no he *ain't*," Rachel said."

"Well, we get rooms for tonight. Where *vill* you and *die* men be, Hank?" Hihn asked.

"We hadn't planned on staying in Felton tonight, but we'll probably just sleep with the horses and livestock up at the livery. Better pull your machine down there; keep an eye on it."

"Hank, don't know if you heard me, but someone shooting at me put a hole in *der* boiler. 'Bout a foot from *die* top, see it?" Hihn said, pointing.

"Yeah, I see it. Bastards. We'll need more men, I reckon."

"Telegram for them and ask if blacksmith can plug *das* hole. Tell him it must hold three hundred pounds pressure."

Hank set up another rope corral near the stables, and two of the loggers brought up the rest of the stock. Since Hihn and his nieces secured rooms at the Cunningham, Hank bunked out in the Conestoga and his loggers threw bedrolls on the hay stacked inside the livery.

Stryker stayed on the wagon road to Pacific Mills. The narrow-gauge track hugged the trail, crossing it and the San Lorenzo River along the way. The railroad extended two miles north of town; beyond that, crews worked clearing the track line, building trestles, and laying rails on freshly cut ties. Patches of uncompleted rail sections led on up the valley to Boulder Creek.

He dismounted and led the roan into town as dusk began to push out what little light survived in the perpetually shaded valley. Midday allowed but a few short hours of direct sunlight. The heavily forested Santa Cruz Mountains made the valley murky during much of the day; ocean fog further exacerbated the dankness. Even after loggers shaved the mountainsides, the valley floor remained gloomy.

The sign read "Pacific Mills–Pop 386". The town was strung out north-south along the river and the trail ran through it. A quick inspection told Stryker Pacific Mills didn't offer much in the way of food or accommodations. He left the horse with the blacksmith and went to find something for his growling belly.

Coming to "Martha's Good Food" in the middle of town, he decided to give her a try. Stryker paid seventy-five cents for supper to a Chinaman instead, who'd taken over the place and left Martha's sign out front. The small cabin was jammed with loggers and he waited in line before getting a big helping of watery stew slopped on his tray. The coffee poured strong and black and unwashed loggers in soiled clothing provided enough rank odors to mask the smell of the mop-water stew. They threw disapproving glances of suspicion his way and men seated near him at the long table ate in strained silence. Other tables held more talkative workers, albeit in muffled tones and Stryker suspected the room would be more raucous without his presence. Some of the men noticed the .44 hanging low in a well-oiled holster and word spread quickly around the room Stryker was no lumberjack. However, the menacing scowl of the pale-eyed killer suggested to those seated nearby, that although the crowd could overwhelm him, there would be fewer loggers at the breakfast table.

The following morning, Stryker downed two cups of the strong coffee for breakfast and started out on the road to Boulder Creek. Heavy fog hugged the ground and the logging crews took extra time to eat a second stack of flapjacks, being reluctant to bring a giant redwood crashing down through fog. Rail men launched their work day ahead of the loggers, but they also started later than usual.

Stryker guided the roan onto the trail ahead of the crews. Redwood and Douglas fir loomed as tall sentinels lining the road, showing only their trunks through the mist. Tanoak and huckleberry bushes draped in ghostly garments of Spanish moss scraped against horse and rider. Low, thick fog obscured the road and he couldn't see much beyond the bobbing head of the roan. Occasionally, he could hear river water rippling over rocks; however, he held the reins loosely, trusting the horse to stay on the trail. The moisture in the air soon soaked him and his gear, and he questioned his own judgment for starting out in such poor visibility. Chilled, he pulled the heavy jacket tighter and raised his collar snug under his hat to keep his neck dry.

CHAPTER FOURTEEN

An hour on the road and deep in past memories, the mixed-breed didn't notice the fog had thinned, nor did he become aware of the large four-legged figure standing motionless a hundred paces up ahead.

The roan began acting skittish and Stryker quickly returned to the present, his senses sharpened. He pulled the Winchester from its scabbard and eased from the saddle, landing lightly on his feet. After looping the reins over a berry bush, he chambered a round. He crouched forward with his forefinger lightly on the trigger, front stock cradled in his left hand.

A few more paces and the shadow took shape. It was a deer, a big stag with a huge rack. It stood facing the side of the road, horns lowered, threatening, ready for attack. The buck seemed so focused on what was on the ground it didn't notice the approaching man. But as Stryker came closer, he saw that the animal bled from several grave wounds. Its sides heaved with each labored breath and blood sprayed in snorts from a gaping wound on its muzzle. The muzzle ripped open, hung down in a large bloody flap. The nape of its neck had numerous bite and claw marks. And more long gashes ran down its shoulder. Stryker wondered if the stag remained frozen not so much because of the object of its attention, but rather, if it tried to move it would collapse.

Stryker shifted his attention away from the stag and looked for the attacker. He saw it soon enough. A young mountain lion, its tongue lolling from a bloodied mouth, lay not ten feet away, hidden by brush, the reason why he hadn't seen it before. Countless puncture wounds checkered the cougar's chest and abdomen. Shallow breaths barely lifted its sides. Its eyes, glazed over and sightless, opened slowly and then closed. The cougar's head settled to the ground.

The sight of the magnificent stag, standing mutilated and bleeding, yet victorious, caused Stryker to pause. The animal staggered forward but almost lost its balance. It waited, as if to accept whatever fate the man now brought. Stryker raised the carbine, put the end of the barrel a couple inches from the stag's right eye and pulled the trigger.

The roan had stayed calm; perhaps sensing the cat posed no threat. Stryker threw a boot in the stirrup, gripped the saddle horn, and paused with one foot still on the ground. Beyond the saddle, he saw a shaft of sunlight illuming a single redwood. The giant tree stretched upward three hundred feet to touch a patch of brilliant blue sky.

"They're something, ain't they?" Hank Ledbetter appeared on foot out of the mist, a good forty paces down the road. "Some of them big ones was here when Christ walked the earth."

Stryker, surprised he hadn't heard the logger earlier, pulled his boot from the stirrup, turned to face Ledbetter, and leveled the Winchester.

"Easy, mister. Got yourself a good-looking buck there," Hank said, walking closer. He brushed past Stryker and knelt to count the points. "Heard the shot. Figured you might've been huntn' breakfast." Damn! What happen to him?"

"Cougar. Over there." Stryker pointed with the carbine. "You haven't trailed me to talk about nature." The barrel casually swung back toward Hank.

"Mister Hihn sent me. They tried to kill him. He's been shot."

"I'm off the payroll."

"Said to tell you he needs you."

"Need is not enough."

"Hihn said he'd make it worth your while. Look, Stryker, my boys are just loggers. We ain't gunmen."

"Not for hire." Stryker turned and jammed the carbine in its boot.

"Miss Kahla says you owe her."

"Tell her I paid up."

"Tell her yourself."

"Tell me what?" Kahla said, leading two horses into view.

"I told Kahla to hold up behind one of them big trees when we heard the shot," Hank interjected. "Fog helped too. Ain't often seen fog this thick. And quiet, real quiet. Don't seem natural."

"Tell me what?" Kahla repeated, bringing Hank's gelding and her gray mare next to the roan.

"That Mister Stryker don't owe you," Hank said, locking eyes with Stryker.

Kahla knew convincing Stryker would be difficult. Hihn, in talking with her and Rachel after Stryker left, had made that clear. When the two wanted to ride out to bring him back, their uncle warned them. "He's got a hole in 'im. Ain't you nor nobody gonna fill it. And that man's been chiseled outta granite. Anyone tries to get close will get cut on the sharp edges." She'd do her best.

"I'm the one who insisted we ride up to pull your raggedy ass off that hill. Weren't for me, you'd be animal shit. And I'm the one who had a hand in waking you from the coma." Kahla stared icily at Stryker, holding his glare. "You . . . owe . . . me."

Without warning the horses reared, squealing and white-eyed. Stryker dodged the roan's flailing hooves and gripped the reins, but the other two horses ripped their straps from Kahla's hands. The gelding spun in unison with the mare and together they raced down the road. The fog swallowed them, and the staccato clopping of their hooves soon grew faint.

"Whoa, whoa. Easy now." Stryker fought the roan. He gave enough slack for the animal to rear, but had it chosen to bolt, one man, or even two, couldn't've held it. However, years with the man gripping the leather had built up trust and Stryker held the reins. Finally, the roan settled on all fours, dancing in a circle, shaking its mane.

"What got into 'em?" Hank stared into the fog as though he could see through it and watch the horses run. "That cougar?"

"Cougar?" Kahla hadn't noticed the big cat. That what killed the . . . hey! What's going . . .?"

It started with a low moaning, down deep in the ground. Birds took flight, squawking and flapping wings to gain altitude. The ground began a slow rolling motion, picking up intensity, and escalating into a violent shaking action back and forth.

"Earthquake!" Hank yelled, spreading his legs, struggling to stay on his feet.

Stryker threw himself on the roan, wrapping his arm around its neck. Both horse and man balanced themselves on splayed legs. Instinct and Stryker's firm grasp kept the big horse from bolting as the ground trembled.

Kahla tottered onto one leg and fell. She hit the road hard with an arm pinned under her side. "Huummppff!" Her wind whooshed out, causing her diaphragm to spasm. She lifted herself upright and tried to talk, but she could only mouth the words, "I can't breathe."

Hank dropped to all fours and crawled over.

It seemed to drag on longer, but the earthquake ended after just fifteen seconds.

"You all right?" Hank lifted Kahla to her feet.

"Uhh . . . yes." Kahla finally got her wind back. She tried a deep breath but stopped, raising her hand to her side. "Ohhh . . . no . . . my ribs; they hurt."

"You mighta' broke one. You landed hard on that arm." Hank gently brushed the dirt from her clothing.

She turned to Stryker. "No doubt if you came upon us like this, you'd just ride on by," she said, grimacing. "But you've got unpaid debts."

Stryker pulled the reins over the roan's ears and swung in the saddle. He shifted his seat and leaned down, holding out an arm.

Hank crouched in front of Kahla and made a stirrup with clasped hands. Aided by both men, she climbed behind Stryker. She wrapped her arms around his waist and gave him a small squeeze. The little squeeze deepened his already foul mood.

"We would have to bag a nice buck with no way to haul it." Hank groused briskly walking beside the roan. "Another gol-durned earthquake."

"What do you mean another?" Kahla asked. She groaned and rested her forehead against Stryker's back. "We have to go slower, or I have to rest. My side hurts worse."

"Been gettin' these little ones since I been here. Thought I *was* used to 'em, but not *that* one." Hank glanced up at Kahla. "You hurtin' bad?"

Stryker reined slower.

"An' these damn boots ain't made for hiking neither," Hank added.

"You said Hihn got shot." Stryker said it like a command to explain the shooting, rather than a statement of fact.

"First day out with the Steam donkey. Damn thing worked good too. He was showing me and a couple of boys how to run it. Pulled them logs up that mountain like they wuz toothpicks. We didn't know he wuz shot 'til he fell off the donkey, and we saw blood on his back. Shot him twice. He's in a bad way."

"Where's Hihn now?"

"Got some of the boys guarding him at the Cunningham House; Rachel's in with 'im. Doc dug a bullet outta his chest. Other'n went clean through his side. Might make it, might not."

"Who did it?" Stryker put the reins in his left hand.

"Heyman Ekard." Kahla lifted her head and spat the name in Stryker's ear. "If he didn't do it, the sneaky coward ordered it. Damn." She groaned, laying her head on Stryker's shoulder.

"Tell me more about Ekard." Stryker squinted ahead, occasionally glancing around and behind . . . and thinking he should have ridden faster to San Francisco.

"Ekard," Hank repeated. He scrunched up his face, indicating thoughtful study. "Well, don't know too much about him; showed up after the Union Pacific strike. Heared some of them anarchists stirred up things over there. Men done some shootin'. Maybe he's one of them. Gives speeches tellin' everybody they need to rise up an' take over everything. Shoot them that tries to stop 'em. Wears them square glasses like he's real smart."

"Renard said they outnumbered your men, ten to one. Ekard's men?"

"There's some showed up when Ekard did. Most of 'em lumber boys from outfits here already. Ekard and this other feller-don't know his name-gets men all riled up; march around town at night with torches shoutn' stuff and shootin' off guns. You get enough liquor in a man; he'll get rowdy and do all kinds 'a dumb shit. Sorry, Kahla. Anyway, everybody knew Hihn wuz bringin' in that donkey. Weren't havn' no trouble 'til that Ekard bunch showed up."

"Shoot the bastard, Stryker." Kahla said to his shoulder.

"And the donkey?" Irritated at the prospect of being used, Stryker shifted forward to spit, causing Kahla to moan again. The more he thought about it, the darker his mood got. He didn't have a dog, or a donkey, in the fight.

"Me and my boys fired 'er up the next mornin'. Had rifles out 'round it so as to pre-vent trouble. We sure liked watch'n it pull them logs. Ox just stood there watch'n too. They ain't complainin'. That's what we wuz doin' when Kahla here came up to get me to find you."

"Renard?" Stryker growled.

"He's a funny fellow. Knows the steam donkey inside out, but some days he shows up, some days he don't."

"Hank, get Hihn and the girls out of Felton. Move them where they'll be out of the way while we settle things here," Stryker ordered.

"All right. What're you gonna do about Ekard?" Ledbetter asked, looking up at Stryker.

"Kill him."

Kahla gave Stryker another squeeze.

Stryker wrenched Kahla's hands loose, twisted around to grab the coat, and slung her off. Hank saw Stryker's move and reacted in time to catch the falling woman.

"Put her on the train to Felton." Stryker heeled the roan to a gallop and vanished into the fog.

Hank lowered Kahla to her feet, his arm circling her waist. Looking at the fog that had swallowed Stryker, he said, "Your friend has some tough bark on him."

"How far to town, Hank?"

"Half mile."

The fog lifted two miles south of Pacific Mills. The ride allowed Stryker to weigh what to do back in Felton. Hihn would stay at the hotel if he were as bad as Ledbetter said. And his arriving alone, without Hank or Kahla, would give him a freer hand, he told himself. A little guilt, but then again, maybe not. Anyway, if he got bush-whacked riding in . . . Kahla's safer coming in with Hank. He tried to convince himself that was the reason he threw Kahla to the ground.

Stryker entered Felton and pulled up in front of Cooper's Saloon. Still mid-afternoon, the loggers and mill workers had not yet gathered at the town's favorite watering hole. He looped the reins on a rail, leaped up the three steps, and pushed through the bats' wings. Moving to one side, he backed against a wall until his eyes adjusted. Upturned chairs ringed around table tops in front, and a bar with liquor bottles on shelves behind it ran down the wall on his right. Left of him, stairs led up to the second level where doors numbering one thru nine ran along an L-shaped balcony. An old man in ragged overalls was methodically slapping chairs onto the rough floorboards while another younger man wearing a white shirt, dungarees, and apron cleaned the bar top with a rag.

A woman, who looked to be in her late thirties, came through a doorway beyond the bar. "We're not open. Come back in a half hour."

She sashayed across the floor, one hand resting authoritatively on a swaggering hip. Her red-satin dress bounced with each step as she approached Stryker. He noticed her make-up and hairstyle seemed out of touch with the garish dress. Her auburn hair, parted on one side, hung straight to her shoulders. She had dabbed her prominent cheek-bones with pale rouge and red lipstick, applied sparingly, glistened on her thin lips. The ends of her mouth dipped slightly, suggesting a hint of malice to Stryker.

"Didn't you hear . . .?"

Stryker flipped a chair to the floor, sat down, and crossed his feet at the ankles. He leaned his head back and looked at the woman from under the brim of his Stetson.

His ghostly steel grays momentarily froze her. She recovered quickly. "We don't need more strangers in town stirring up trouble."

"Bring a beer and tell me about the other strangers, Miss . . ." Stryker waited for a name.

"Claire." She half-turned to the bar. "Ed, bring Mister . . ." Claire played along.

"Stryker."

"A beer," Claire told the man in the white shirt. Then back to Stryker, "So you're not with them?"

"Depends on the 'them'."

Claire studied the menacing features of the man across from her. "Outside troublemakers, they appeared here after the rail strike. Figured they called in more guns after two of their own got killed with their pants down."

"Not your man, and I don't truck with men who drop their pants."

Claire cocked her head and crinkled her eyes. Corners of the firmly set lips rose ever so slightly.

Ed plopped the mug down, spilling beer on the table. Stryker swiped the spilt beer off the table with his hand. He lifted the glass, sipped it, and said, "You the Cooper who owns this place?"

"No. The proprietor's not here."

"Big word for a saloon hussy."

"You needn't be so free with your compliments. I'm choosy. And you haven't made the list."

"And these new men in town?"

"Brag about being members of the International Workers something or other Party."

"Call themselves socialbuls," the old man chimed in, throwing a chair on the floor.

"Socialists. They're called socialists, Cletus," Claire corrected.

"Like cockroaches." Stryker said into his glass, taking another sip.

"Crawling all over." Claire blandly replied.

"How many are there?"

"Don't know for sure. Seven or eight, I guess."

"How much for the beer?" Stryker rose to his feet.

"On the house."

Stryker flipped a coin on the table. "Pay my own way." He started for the door.

"You could make the list if you tried," Claire said, after the doors swung closed behind him.

CHAPTER FIFTEEN

Stryker led the roan to the livery where he paid for curry and feed before heading to the Cunningham. A few sips of warm beer had no effect on the stiffness from the damp weather. He walked briskly to flush the chill from his bones. Railroad tracks ran along a log flume which would get little use when narrow gauge rails ran all the way up to Boulder Creek. Hihn's steam donkey was just another player in Felton's progress. Like a lot of communities, steps into the future are pushed and pulled from many sides, yet eventually they grind forward, often with bloodshed. Now, after being dragged into Felton's struggle, things didn't sit well with the mixed-breed.

He left the main street and passed a group of one story, white clapboarded buildings, until he came to the two-story hotel, painted white as well, and trimmed in forest green. He climbed four broad steps, entered through double glass doors, and stopped at a Dutch doorway punched in the entryway wall. A flat ornate shelf holding a register and pen atop the bottom half functioned as the front desk. Large European rugs covered most of the polished wooden floors throughout the entrance hall, and the spacious sitting room beyond it. The brightly painted white interior walls were also trimmed in forest green, with furniture and window dressings reflecting the owner's attempt to style the hotel as an Alpine resort.

"Good afternoon, sir. Name's J.F. Can I be of service?" Looking uneasy, a portly middle-aged man who wore an olive suede vest over a white shirt, and with burgundy suspenders buttoned onto gray suede knickers said, "Are you seeking accommodations for the night?" He fidgeted with the sign-in book.

"German, called Hihn. What room?" Stryker asked curtly.

"Sir, I'm afraid we don't . . ."

"Not here to kill *him*." Stryker rested his hand on the butt of the Peacemaker. "Won't ask again."

"I believe you'll find him upstairs. He's in room eight." He leaned over the Dutch door's ledge and watched Stryker stride through the sitting room and go up the stairs. "Ah damn . . . the guards."

"Stryker!" Rachel had just come from the kitchen to the dining room when she saw him on the stairs.

Stryker climbed the stairs and rounded the corner to come face to face with two men with shotguns in the hallway. They tried to whip the scatterguns toward him, but Stryker drew the .44 and sent a slug crashing into the shoulder of the closest man. The bullet spun him into the second man, whacking the man's jaw with the gun barrel, toppling him like felled timber to the floor. The shotgun dropped from the wounded man's hands and clattered harmlessly to the carpeted floor. Clutching his bloody shoulder, he slumped to his knees.

When the shooting started, Rachel dropped the bowl of soup and ran to the stairs. She raced up, taking two at a time. "Stryker, stop! They're our men. Ralph! Jonah! Stryker's with us!" Rachel screamed, leaping over the last step. She came up behind the mixed-breed as he eased the Colt's hammer forward.

"Christ! Do you have to shoot everyone?" Rachel said breathlessly.

"Didn't kill him," Stryker said.

She pushed past him to the two guards on the floor. Kneeling beside Ralph, she asked, "You hurt bad?"

"Got me in the shoulder," Ralph groaned. "Jonah ain't been shot.

Who the hell is he?" Ralph asked, looking up at Stryker coming toward them.

"Stryker. My uncle hired him on the way here. I thought he'd left us, but Kahla must have found him. Say, where *is* Kahla?" Rachel stood up and faced him.

"On a train. Fell when the earthquake hit. Hurt her ribs." Stryker holstered the Peacemaker. Looking past Rachel, he asked, "Hihn in there?" The door numbered 8 cracked open. A man's face peaked through and before Rachel answered, Stryker banged the door against the peeper's forehead.

"Ow! Dammit!" The man stepped back and pulled the door open. "You could've just asked. Shit." He rubbed the growing knot on his forehead and inspected his fingers for blood. Three men behind him held pistols at the ready.

"For Christ's sake! All of you put away the guns!" Rachel shouted, shoving her way through the door. "Help Ralph and Jonah in here. One of you go for the doctor." "You and you," she said, jabbing a stiff fore-finger, "pick up the shotguns and stand by the door." Rachel barked commands like a drill sergeant and the men jumped to obey.

Stryker moved inside the room and saw cards, chips, and money on the card table surrounded by kicked over chairs. No bed and no Hihn. He turned to Rachel. "Clever."

Rachel guided Ralph from the door to a chair and eased the bloody shirt off his shoulder. One of the men produced a pocketknife to cut away the red undershirt. She examined the entry wound carefully, then a larger exit hole in his back. "Well, it went through. Made a mess in back. But it looks like it might have missed the bone." Rachel scrunched up her face close to the exit wound. "I don't see fragments back here." She straightened and said, "Just sit there and let it bleed. If the doctor doesn't come in ten minutes, have one of the men hold a clean cloth on the back wound."

"Stryker, come with me." Rachel wiped her hands on a dry section of Ralph's cut off undershirt.

Kahla's, and now Rachel's mood changed since the shooting of their uncle. Stryker thought they now seemed to act with a sense of purpose, a solemnity akin to his own temperament, but that was not necessarily welcomed. Cognizant of his own surliness and failure to adjust, he didn't want a world full of people like himself. He knew he demanded a wide berth and ample allowances. However, tragically violent blows throughout his life had shaped and defined him. One thing he wouldn't change, one thing he couldn't change, was paying back good will afforded to him by others.

Rachel abruptly walked out of the room, turned left, and marched to the end of the hall. She knocked softly on room 16's door and while waiting for the door to open, returned Stryker's hard glare with one of her own. It told Stryker this room next to the outside stairs held her uncle. The door cracked open.

"It's me, Rachel."

"We heard a shot." A man towering a good six and a half feet opened the door wider.

"Stryker's back. Shot Ralph by mistake."

The lumberjack, wearing a checkered red and black tent of a shirt, swung the door open. "How's Ralph?" The huge man glowered at Stryker entering behind Rachel.

"Should be okay. Bullet went through the shoulder. Doctor's comin'," Rachel saw Buster's scowl. "Ralph and Jonah thought he was one of them and . . . lucky no one died. Stryker's good with a gun," she added, arcing her eyebrows to warn—don't challenge him.

"Stryker." From his wrought iron bed, Hihn heard Rachel call his name. "Stryker thanks for . . ." Hihn coughed weakly. "I want to sit up."

Buster scooted past Rachel, dug his big hands under the German's shoulders, and lifted him upright. Hihn groaned in agony. He took a moment to recover. Although the pain never left his face, he continued, "Doc said I could get pneumonia. Says get to *die* coast." He coughed again and then went on. "John Cass, got house by . . . sea. Been trying years . . . have me come there. Town called Cayucos. Telegraph him. Go to Santa Cruz and do it." Hihn motioned to be laid back down.

"Send your man Hank with them," Stryker said, bending down to look out the window. "Or your brother."

"No Stryker, you go. Take the girls. Leave them at the hotel. Come back soon." Hihn closed his eyes. "I must rest."

"Get me a room on this floor. I'll be back tonight." Stryker walked out and passed the doctor entering room 8.

Stopping at the station ticket window, Stryker bought tickets for the nine o'clock train leaving the next morning to Santa Cruz. The ticket master told him he'd have to purchase return tickets for the next morning in Santa Cruz. He'd stepped away from the window when he heard three loud whistle blasts.

The train from Ben Lomond rounded into view, coming straight on with its engine snorting a white mustache of steam. When it finally came to a full stop, Hank hopped off a passenger car that rolled behind three flatbeds stacked with logs. He swiveled around quickly and extended his arms up to help Kahla down from the coach. In obvious distress, she carefully rested both feet on each step before cautiously reaching a foot down to the next one. She got to the platform with no small effort and looked up to see Stryker.

"You throw me off the damn horse and now you come greeting me?" Kahla groaned. The pain in her ribs gated the words to a whisper.

"You're catching the nine o'clock train to Santa Cruz in the morning." Stryker flashed the three tickets in his hand, stuffed the tickets back in his shirt pocket, and walked off the platform.

"My ribs hurt like hell. Thanks for asking," Kahla said under her breath.

"Doc's at the hotel." Stryker didn't bother looking back.

"Did he say the doctor was at the hotel?" Kahla asked Ledbetter. "And why am I going to Santa Cruz?"

"I wonder who's using the other two tickets." Hank said, watching Stryker lead the roan toward the livery.

The next morning three people waited at the station for the nine o'clock train, Rachel, Kahla, and Ledbetter, who carried the girls' bags. Hank's resentment toward the tall gunman abated after Rachel informed him that Stryker had recommended *he* escort the sisters to Santa Cruz. Rachel told him she didn't think Stryker was vying for Kahla's affection.

"Throwing her off a horse hardly seems affectionate." Hank agreed, watching Stryker come up the street. "That man's a threat to our lives."

The ninety-minute train ride to Santa Cruz ended at water's edge of the Pacific Ocean. The couplers jolting together when the train slowed, and jerking apart when it sped up, prompted corresponding groans from Kahla. No matter how hard she tried, she could never find a position to ease her pain. The doctor, who examined her after tending to the injured Ralph, said she had cracked or broken ribs. Other than whiskey he had no pain medication, "but they had cocaine powder in Santa Cruz."

They found the telegraph office near the wharf in Santa Cruz and sent a telegram to John Cass. While waiting for a reply, Stryker took Kahla to the Douglas House, a red-roofed, wooden hotel resting on a hill overlooking the beach. Rachel said she had to make a visit to a photography shop and hurried off to hail a carriage.

"I'm staying in here," Kahla told Stryker, as she entered the room. "Why did Rachel go to the photography shop?" She lay down on the four-poster bed and positioned the large silk pillows. "Please go to the apothecary and get the pain medication." She tugged at his sleeve. "Falling off that horse made it worse," she said tactfully.

Stryker bought his return ticket to Felton and followed the station-master's directions to the drugstore. When he got back to the room, he found Rachel sitting on the bed beside Kahla, stroking her forehead. Stryker handed the bag of chocolate-covered cocaine tablets to Rachel and she gave one to Kahla with a glass of water.

"Your room is next to this one." Rachel extended an arm with a key dangling on her forefinger. She pointed at the wall behind him and then canted her finger at him. The key slid to his palm.

"I'll check the telegraph office tomorrow before catching the train." Stryker's habit of talking while walking away seemed expected, because neither woman reacted to his dismissiveness.

"Would you like me to have a meal brought up?" Rachel asked Kahla.

"No."

The girls watched as Stryker closed the door behind him. "I was hoping he would've said yes so he could choke on it," Kahla groused.

After breakfast the next morning, Stryker stopped at the telegraph office and learned Cass had wired a reply welcoming the Hihns to Cayucos. With a two hour wait ahead before train time, he decided to get fresh air along the wharf. A coastal steamer lay docked at pier's end, making a brief stopover on its way down the coast to San Diego. Disembarking passengers hurried past, trailed by porters pushing handcarts loaded with Saratoga trunks, and other baggage. Those boarding waited by the gangplank, then as Stryker got farther out on the pier, they began filing up the ramp. Men followed with their luggage. He stopped about three-fourths along the pier and idly watched them load. Occasionally, a wave swell would catch his attention and he'd watch it roll by until it broke.

A breeze began to blow, bringing with it a chill. Stryker buttoned his coat and pulled his hat down tighter. The steamer, called the "Eureka" of the Pacific Coast Steamship Company, swayed gently with the swells marching toward shore, its steel hull groaning against the pier. The Captain, wearing a navy-blue uniform sporting eagle wings over gold stripes and accompanied by two junior officers in whites, welcomed the boarding passengers. Stryker pulled off his hat, ran a hand through his hair, and leaned back against the pier railing. He hooked a boot heel on the lowest rail, rested his elbow on the top flat board, and thought about a cup of hot coffee.

Halfway between the boarding ramp and the ship's bow, a solitary figure stood by the ship's safety rail, a woman. A woman with a gray wool shawl slung carelessly around her shoulders. She looked rail thin yet stood tall, arms hanging at her sides. Her brunette hair, parted on one side and swept behind an ear, hung straight to her slender shoulders. Her dark eyes-too far away to see the true color-set above prominent cheekbones, stared at the man leaning on the railing.

The last of the passengers boarded and two seamen winched the ramp up from the pier. Mooring lines were pulled from the four piles and thrown on board while the anchor chain rattled up from the sea.

Stryker eventually let his eyes wander away from the boarding procession to run along the ship's railing to the female figure. The way she stood, the elegant lines that cut into a blue sky behind her, reminded him of the woman he'd known in Egalitaria. Morgan—she reminded him of Morgan Bickford, the woman he'd worked for, the woman he'd fought with, the woman . . . who'd shared his bed.

The woman at the rail looked so strikingly similar. Damn. But the Morgan he'd known, the Morgan for whom the town was originally named, had been shot. Dead. Or so, that's what her teenage son had claimed–a pronouncement which earned the boy a busted nose.

But the woman kept staring at him.

He shoved himself from the rail. The breeze hit his face, and he squinted, blinking several times to see clearly. Standing up to his full height, Stryker squared himself toward her.

The steamer crept forward; the statuesque figure still looked at him, but from a growing distance. He watched until he could no longer see her, until he could no longer see the ship.

Stryker stopped at the ticket office to see where the steamer was headed. When asked about the passenger manifest, the ticket master told him that list was in San Francisco. He only had the list of those boarding in Santa Cruz.

Stryker went back to the hotel and up to the nieces' room. "Cass wired. Said you and your uncle were welcome in Cayucos. You'll like it there." He turned and left.

Kahla started to ask what he'd meant by his last remark, but asked Rachel why she went to the photography shop instead.

"I got a solution they use. Might come in handy."

"Well, what the *hell* did he mean, I'll like it there?" Kahla asked.

"I don't really know. Strange man." The girls stared at the closed door for several long minutes.

Stryker went downstairs and had two cups of black coffee in the dining room. He left the hotel without any farewells to the nieces, walked to the train station, and boarded the Southern Pacific train for Felton.

Stryker chose a bench seat at the rear of the coach, his back against the wall. Only six other passengers boarded the car coupled to the Shay's tender. The rest got in coaches farther back from the smoke-belching engine. A man and woman sat the nearest to him, four rows ahead. Left alone, he had time to reflect on Morgan.

Other than now believing she might be alive, not much changed. He knew it would be highly unlikely their paths would cross again. Leaving Bickford that night may have been enough for her to survive his jinx and the gunshot. If he tried to find her and succeeded, that might just finish her off. Stryker couldn't bring himself to dwell on the unknown, but the jinx that left others in graves had stalked him for too many years, and no matter how illogical it seemed, he just couldn't shake the thing.

CHAPTER SIXTEEN

Stryker looked out both sides of the coach before he rose and got off opposite the station. Keeping the train between him and town, he walked around the end car and crossed the tracks. Mid-morning fog still hung heavy and damp, limiting visibility to less than a hundred yards. He walked behind a row of buildings, making it to the rear stairs of the Cunningham Hotel undetected.

When he reached the second-floor door, the two decoy guards rose as if to challenge him, but neither made the mistake of bringing a gun to bear again. Ralph's replacement had obviously been warned by Jonah, still guarding the door, not to threaten the quick shooting mixed-breed. Stryker rapped his knuckles on the door to Hihn's room and twisted the doorknob. Buster leapt from his chair to answer, but Stryker opened the door first.

"Mister Stryker, you're back." The overweight, forty-something nurse rose to greet him as he crossed the floor to Hihn's bed. "He's feeling better, perhaps well enough to travel, I think." She smiled at the German. "What's the news about Cayucos?" she asked, bending over Hihn to straighten his pillow, treating him to ample cleavage.

"You telegram Cass?" Hihn pulled himself upright, coming within an inch of plowing the fleshy fissure with his nose.

"Said to come . . . and how's here?" Stryker sat in a chair by the bed, rocked it back on two legs, and propped a boot against the iron frame.

"Hank's running crew. Half are logging, other half guarding. It's no way to make a profit," Hihn grumbled. Worrying about money was a sign he felt better.

Buster interjected. "The outta' town troublemakers organize marches through town. When they're not doin' that, they're buying drinks in Cooper's, fanning the flames. Only a matter of time 'fore they hit us again."

"Get him on a train to Santa Cruz," Stryker told Buster. He turned to Hihn. "Your nieces are at the Douglas House near the pier."

"Stryker," Hihn said, "*der* man who shot me, Ekard's cohort, watch out for him. He buys *die* men whiskey, gets them yelling words outside Cooper's. And he shot me from *der* alley. Even in the dark–I could see it was him all right. He is not tall; stout though, got black hair like yours, wears velvet vest. Bill . . . that's his name, Buster?"

"Yep, Bill. Thinks he's a real lady's man. Mister Hihn won't let me kill him," Buster growled.

"I need you here. Besides, *der* Sheriff should arrest him. Just be careful, Stryker."

"Gonna talk to Ledbetter." Stryker dropped his boot from the bed and slammed the chair legs to the floor. He stood and started for the door. He gripped the doorknob and turned to Hihn. "You owe me six-hundred and forty dollars."

"Six-hundred!" Hihn coughed and then groaned in pain.

"I'll let forty slide, for now." Stryker opened the door.

What money Hihn saved on labor with the steam donkey went to pay the guards. He'd complained to Ledbetter the extra guards caused him to operate at a loss. Although concerned he may not meet payroll for the crew, Hihn knew one man had to be paid before all others.

"You *vill* get *das* money before we leave," Hihn said, slumping against the pillow.

Stryker walked out and passed the two guards, who warily kept their eyes on him until he disappeared down the stairs. Downstairs he met J.F. Cunningham, the Tyrolean owner, in the foyer. "Give me a room on the second floor."

J.F. rounded a potted plant and entered a side door to his office. He threw open the Dutch door and slapped a key to room ten on the counter. Stryker pocketed the key, ignored the register signing, and left.

He headed up the street to Cooper's Saloon, figuring it too early for crews to be quenching dry throats and aiming to see Claire alone. Morning fog had retreated to lurk by the river and he saw locals on Felton's main street, going about their daily chores. The saw mill at the far end of town interrupted street clatter with intermittent high-pitched whines, as the big saw ripped through logs. No one cast suspicious looks his way, at least none he noticed.

"Well, you're back. Heard you left town," Claire said, as Stryker broke through the swinging doors. She salted cheerfulness in the greeting, hinting she was glad to see him. "Coffee?" She sat two cups on a table and waved him over.

"Just information," Stryker answered, looking around the saloon. He saw they were alone. "Ekard and his man, Bill, tell me about 'em."

"Bill and three or four other men come in here. Preach and agitate. Ekard, don't see much of him. Stays at a boarding house a little ways south of town. I see him going back and forth to the telegraph office." Clair pushed a cup in front of Stryker. "Now that Bill fellow, he comes in here. He's here now, upstairs with one of the girls. He's taking a liking to her. Slaps her around, then does what he does. She doesn't seem to mind, and he buys a lot of drinks."

"What room?"

Claire had raised her cup but placed it back on the table. "What you gonna do?"

Stryker answered into his cup. "He tried to kill a man who owes me money." He tasted the coffee and lowered the cup. "What room?"

He pushed from the table and headed for the stairs.

"All right, you don't have to open every door. At the top, first on your left, just talk to 'im." Claire paused, and then added. "Don't hurt the girl."

Claire stayed seated, rotating the coffee mug with nervous

fingers. A few minutes passed, and a door banged open. A naked Juanita, clutching a robe, ran from the room and scrambled down the stairs, using both hands on the rail. She managed to wrap the robe around her on the way to the bar, where she grabbed a bottle and filled a beer glass with whiskey. Coming to Claire's table, she plopped into a chair. The robe fell open, exposing ample breasts, but Juanita didn't notice. She took a long drink, furrowing her bruised and swollen face tightly. Then she brought the glass to her mouth again.

"What happened?" Claire asked.

Juanita clutched the mug next to her heart . . . nestled between the fleshy mounds. "Bill did his usual foreplay, slapping shit out outta me. I was on top." She sipped the whiskey. "Suddenly this man grabbed my hair and jerked me back. It must have hurt Bill's 'you-know', because he yowled in pain. And that's when he rammed a big fork thing through Bill's mouth."

"A fork?" Claire interrupted. She straightened, bracing herself.

"Not a regular fork. It had three points, one long, middle one. It went in his mouth, the other two alongside his face—the long one must've gone clean through his neck. Bill's eyes got as big as pancakes and he bit down on it. The man jiggled that thing back and forth, Bill's head bobbing up and down like a church deacon's." She set the mug on the table and stared at it between her open hands, palms turned up, as if imploring the whiskey to tell the rest. "When he pulled it out, it was dripping blood. Bill started choking; throwing up, then he just stopped. I got outta there. Left that man cleaning the thing on Bill's shirt." She lifted her face to Claire's.

"Juanita." Claire said the name slowly. "We better not repeat what just happened up there."

A door slammed upstairs. Juanita kept her back to the stairs, her face frozen with fear. Claire laid a reassuring hand on the girl's wrist, and watched as Stryker came down the stairs, and walked out the swing doors.

"Clifford!" Claire looked sternly at the girl and lowered her voice. "Juanita. I don't want Bill's friends busting up the place. And that man, you want him after you?" Juanita shook her head no. "Then keep your mouth shut."

The old man in overalls came through the kitchen door and shuffled to their table.

"Cliff, there's a man dead upstairs. You'll need someone to help you. He's a mess," Claire said, eying Juanita.

"What happen to him? How'd he die, Miss Claire?" Clifford wiped his forehead.

"He got something stuck in his throat and choked on it."

Stryker walked out of Cooper's and down to the Felton Livery and Feed. The blacksmith gave him directions to the Hihn cut area, and twenty minutes later, he came out leading the roan, saddled and prancing behind. He mounted up and took the road north again. Keeping an easy canter for about a mile, he slowed to a walk, and then turned west up the steep logging trail. As he climbed alongside the skid logs, laid out horizontally, he passed an oxen team, guarded by men carrying shotguns, pulling a large cut log down to the railroad tracks.

It took a half hour of climbing before he could hear the rattling steam donkey and see puffs of smoke drifting above the trees. Cresting the ridge, he spied the chugging donkey among the pines to his right. Ropes drawn taut behind, tied to sturdy tree trunks, and a rigid cable strung to the front, it seemed like a tortured prisoner stretched out between the pines. As Stryker got closer, he saw a log, two-foot in diameter, crawling up the hill, pulled by the cable. Occasionally the log caught on a rock or stump, and the steam donkey would rise completely off the ground until the log lurched past the impediment.

Hank saw Stryker sitting on the roan, leaning forward with crossed forearms on the saddle horn, and scrambled up to greet him. "It's something, ain't it?" He yelled over the engine's clamor.

"I see why Hihn wanted it."

"Ten oxen couldn't pull them logs up that hill. Allows us to work this side. Ain't another crew up here but us," Hank crowed.

"Where's the other outfits?" Stryker asked, glancing along the ridge to the north.

"They've cut up past Ben Lomond, close to Boulder Creek, 'bout four or five miles up the river, or rail the tracks–if they've laid 'em that far. You goin' up there?" Hank arched his eyebrows.

"Not yet." Stryker returned to watching the steam donkey.

"They're a rough bunch." Hank warned.

"Renard?" Stryker sat up and shifted his weight in the saddle.

"Ain't seen him lately."

Stryker wheeled the roan around and started down the hill. Another crew was bringing up more oxen. They, too, had armed guards. The skid road ended down by the tracks, where men with pike poles rolled logs across a wooden platform. It was level with the flatcars, so logs could be loaded. More armed men stood guard there, and twice during the past week, the loggers had to pull a log off the track to stop the train.

"Hihn's right," Stryker silently admitted. "*Was* a waste of men."

Satisfied with the crew's security, Stryker rode the river trail back to Felton. He swung out of the saddle before entering town, draped the reins over the roan's head, and led it down the street. Dusk had arrived, shaping buildings into oblique outlines against the mountains surrounding Felton. The big rip saw, now quiet, allowed saloon noise to roll up the street without interference. He expected to see groups of citizens gathered outside Cooper's discussing Bill's death and was surprised to find folks carrying on business as usual. He did get nervous glances, though. He always got those. But they were not thrown with suspicion. Until he spied a new coffin leaning against the outside wall of Peterson's Mortuary, he'd started to wonder if the body had been recovered.

The sweet aroma of baked apple pie drifted out an open window as Stryker walked past the Cunningham Hotel. Pastries rarely tempted him, but the prospect of good hot coffee with sausage biscuits made his belly growl. He quickened his pace to the livery.

Claire sat at a table adorned with a candelabra and white linen cloth. The other tables set bare. She looked up when Stryker entered the hotel dining room and waved him to join her.

Stryker laid his jacket over an empty chair and pulled one out next to it. "Fancy dining for a floozy," Stryker said, waving for the waiter. He shouted his order before the young man reached their table. "Coffee and sausage biscuits with gravy."

The waiter stopped, unsure if he should get Claire's order now or turn around.

Claire called him over. "And I'll have your best wine, the chicken, and I haven't made up my mind on anything else. Thank you." The waiter walked away. "You should try their chicken," she said to Stryker.

Stryker scooted back his chair and got to his feet. "Need to wash up."

Buster came down the stairs, missing Stryker, who had just gone in the door marked, "Gents."

"He's back," Claire told Buster as he came up. "He's washing his hands." She tipped her newly delivered wine glass toward the hallway.

"I don't care for him," the big man replied.

"Whatever you do, my friend, do *not* rile him." Claire didn't look at Buster, still standing. She remained staring at the hallway instead.

"Hihn said he's fast. So it wasn't too difficult talking Hihn into taking him instead of me. But he may not be so tough without a gun," Buster growled.

"Buster, get a good look at that man's face. Something evil lurks behind his cold, pale eyes. We thought Bill was tough, but this one killed *him*. Juanita said he used some*thing* on him. Scared her so bad she left—gone—got on a train and left."

"He killed Bill? She saw it? I thought he choked."

"She saw it alright. That's why she left. Here he comes."

Buster turned to greet Stryker approaching the table. He pulled an envelope from his jacket and held it out. "From Hihn. Says you're paid up plus another ten days pay in there."

Stryker pocketed the money and took a seat. He sat back in the chair and lifted the cup of coffee placed on the table while he was gone. "Why the advance pay?"

Buster circled the table and pulled out the empty chair, choosing not to disturb Stryker's coat. He signaled the waiter after being seated and then turned his attention to Stryker. "Hihn wants you with him to Cayucos."

"I'll take care of things here and be on my way."

"Claire?" Buster turned to her for help.

"Mister Stryker, what do you know about anarchists?" She asked.

Stryker shifted his attention to Claire.

Claire paused long enough to realize she wouldn't get an answer. "You killed one this morning."

"Pleasure."

A faint smile turned up the corners of Claire's mouth. She glanced at Buster, then back to Stryker. "President Cleveland sent a small team of investigators out west to try and find out who is behind the recent rash of civil disruptions, railroad strikes, riots, and unsolved killings. Killings in several states, yet seemingly connected politically. I'm a member of that team. Perhaps you'll meet the others later. Buster here," Claire dipped her head at the big man, "has agreed to aid our investigation, although he is not on our team. We know you had a hand in the two deaths on the train, and now this Bill fellow—all anarchists or in their employ, we believe. But we need to get to the leader or leaders. Bill was our best chance. He had begun to talk to Juanita. We paid her well, but he beat her-all for nothing now. To cut to the heart of it, Mister Stryker, we need to get you out of Felton before you kill 'em all."

The three of them sat in silence. Stryker digested the new information while studying the woman. Claire sipped wine and stared back at him. Buster propped both elbows on the table, looking anxiously from one to the other. Neither Stryker nor Claire acknowledged their dinners placed on the table.

"Neville," Claire said, "We also know of your dealings with a man called Bauer," subtly telling Stryker she knew about his past.

Though surprised, Stryker gave no hint of it. Then, she must surely know he was a wanted man back East and still on the run. His muscles tensed. His hand slipped down to drape the butt of the Peacemaker.

Claire saw the arm drop, and she quickly followed with, "We're not here to arrest you. There is some speculation he had something to do with your wife's death. We just need you to let us do our job."

Claire reached for her knife and fork and cut into the chicken. "Let's eat before our food gets cold, shall we?" Seeing no response from Stryker after her first forkful, "I hear Cayucos is by the sea. You'd like it."

Stryker scooted the sausage plate in front of Buster, his eyes still locked on Claire. The big man looked down at the plate, then at Claire, questioning Stryker's move with cocked eyebrows.

"I'll speak to the President about a pardon," Claire said, resting the fork on the linen. "Stryker, you could kill us and half of Felton before you were stopped, but what good would that do?"

Suddenly Stryker jumped to his feet, overturning the chair behind him. Claire covered her mouth with a hand, palm out. Her eyes grew large.

"Eat it," Stryker said through clenched teeth to Buster. And as he turned to leave, "Keep your damn pardon."

"Good God, I thought he was going to shoot us," Claire squeaked after Stryker left.

CHAPTER SEVENTEEN

The following morning Buster carried Hihn downstairs and put him on a baggage cart for the ride to the train station. Stryker ate a hearty breakfast of steak and eggs, and he'd just finished his second cup of the strong black coffee when he heard the train whistle. He picked up his satchel and hotfooted across the station platform as the Shea's wheels spun in place, fighting to gain traction. One by one, front to rear, the rail cars jolted forward, clanking their couplers together. He jumped on the last footstep and clambered up. He ran into Buster coming out the coach door.

"You're late . . . uh, he's laid out on a bench . . .," Buster began.

Stryker pulled the .44 and shoved the barrel in Buster's gut. "You're going to Santa Cruz." Buster backed inside the coach.

"I guess I'm going to Santa Cruz with you, Mister Hihn," Buster said, taking a bench seat opposite the German.

"Thank you, Buster," Hihn replied. "I was thinking it would be a good idea. Where is Stryker?"

"He's right behind you." Looking up at the mixed-breed, Buster said, "He's kind of in a foul mood."

Stryker holstered the .44 and took the rear seat behind Hihn. He leaned back against the wall, stretched out his legs, and shoved the hat brim below his brow. The elderly husband and wife across the aisle decided not to extend a greeting to the unfriendly man.

At quarter past noon, the Southern Pacific rounded the last curve before pulling into Santa Cruz. Stryker tipped his hat brim up with a forefinger when its wheels slowed their clacking cadence. Peering out the side window, he saw the outer edge of the coastal town's buildings coming into view.

A little while later, the station platform appeared with passengers waiting beside porters and baggage carts, some loaded, some empty. Beyond the wooden planks of the platform and clusters of bath houses, he saw blue-grey swells gathering to break in white-foamed rolls along the sandy beach. The train crawled to a stop. Stryker tore his eyes away from the mesmerizing ocean and back to the platform. There, he saw Rachel and Kahla next to a chair on wheels.

Stryker stepped off the train ahead of Hihn and Buster. He scanned the platform, and seeing nothing suspicious, headed toward the sisters. They waved and broke into a short dash, ending with two skip steps. Kahla, heavily *medicated,* ran faster and raised outstretched arms for Stryker, but seeing his usual expression, dropped them and stopped running.

Rachel moved past Kahla, who stood frozen in awkward indecision a few feet from him. "Where's our uncle?" A concerned frown chased the smile off her face.

"Coming. Do you have a chair for him?"

"Yes, how . . .?"

"Buster. Roll it over there," Stryker hooked a thumb toward the last coach.

Several passengers disembarked before Buster appeared in the doorway, carrying Hihn. The big man adjusted his burden after side-stepping through the door and spied the chair. "They brought a chair for you, I guess." Then he grunted, "Thank God for that." He took three jarring steps down to the platform.

Rachel ran back for the chair and wheeled it toward Buster and Hihn.

"Are you going to Cayucos too?" Kahla asked.

Stryker nodded.

"Sea air should do you good." Kahla shuffled around Stryker to go greet her uncle.

Buster settled Hihn into the chair and covered him with the same blanket used on the train. Hihn, grimacing in pain, asked, "You get tickets, Rachel?"

"I got two cabins, six-dollars each, to Cayucos on a Pacific Coast Steamship. Leaves at seven-thirty tonight."

"Good, we can . . ." Hihn stopped and coughed until he spewed bloody mucus into his handkerchief.

"Let's go to the hotel. And, we should have a doctor look at you before we get on that boat," Rachel said, covering her own mouth.

A little after seven that night, Buster moved Hihn into one of the steamer's cabins. Kahla and Rachel settled in another adjoining Hihn's. A door between them was left unlocked for their convenience.

"Buster, tell Hank to inform us *vith der* logging. I want to know about *der* donkey. Thanks for your help." Hihn lay back on the bunk.

"Reckon, I'll be going then." But the big man remained standing in place, nervously rotating his hat brim in huge rugged hands.

"Buster, tell Hank to pay you an extra ten dollars. Tell him it's Hihn's orders," Rachel said, glancing at her uncle.

Hihn weakly nodded his approval.

Stryker chose not to stay in Hihn's cabin, even though an extra bunk had been brought in. Instead, he located a smaller room down the passageway on the same deck level. Other than leering gapes at the sisters from sailors, Stryker saw no threat from the crew or other passengers, who were mostly families. The door between Hihn and the girls remained ajar, and with their outside doors firmly secured, Hihn didn't object to Stryker sleeping in another room.

The room, tiny even by ship standards, had a drop-down berth, a straight-back chair, and a small writing table attached to the opposite wall which was covered, like the rest of the room, with soiled brown-flowered paper. A lit lamp attached to the wall over the table bathed the interior in soft yellow. Stryker noticed, with a grunt of irritation, that the table was in the only area not lit by the lamp, being precisely positioned in the shadow of the lamp base. He pulled the bed down and picked up a day-old newspaper stuck in the blanket. He took off his boots, lay back on the bed, and began reading the *San Francisco Examiner*.

Hearing two very soft knocks on the door, Stryker lowered the newspaper and reached for the Colt.

"It's me, Rachel."

Her voice sounded hushed. She held her mouth near the door.

"It's unlocked," Stryker answered, slipping the gun under his pillow.

Rachel turned the doorknob and opened the door just wide enough to slip in. Once inside, she held the doorknob, pressed a palm against the door, and eased it shut. She turned and looked around the small cabin with exaggerated inspection, "Luxurious stateroom."

Stryker swung his foot down and shoved the chair at her. If Rachel noticed his reading, she kept it to herself. She sat in the offered chair.

"When you went to find Renard in San Jose, where did you go?"

"Curious about anything particular?"

"Renard. He disappears at odd times. And he's been acting funny, as if his mind is somewhere else." She paused and asked again, "Where'd you go?"

"He smokes opium," Stryker stated flatly, his eyes narrowing.

"You're sure?" Rachel asked. "Oh, my God." Then with resignation, "So in San Jose you *did* go to an opium den looking for him."

Stryker sat up and pulled on his boots. He regretted too late now, telling Rachel about Renard.

"You leaving? No, wait." She laid a gentle hand on Stryker's shoulder. "My uncle came to America after reading Karl May's western stories. He wanted to see the American West. Then he learned of the steam donkey and thought he could make a name for himself and, of course, money."

Stryker leaned forward, elbows on knees, listening.

"Renard's always been trouble. My uncle has had to rescue him time after time, often at great cost. Now, if he has sunk into that awful indulgence, if he's betrayed his brother to get it, I want you to put him on a train to never come back or kill him."

"Betrayed Hihn." Stryker said, staring at the floor, thinking.

"Heard talk, Hank and others. Kahla doesn't know."

Stryker chose not to let Rachel know he'd kill Renard for nothing. "Pay?"

Rachel smiled and said, "Fifty dollars to get him away from here, twenty-five to kill him. Deal?" She rose to her feet and held out her hand. "Then you can go back to reading your paper."

They shook hands. When Stryker began to withdraw his, Rachel squeezed harder, held his eyes with her own. "This is between us." She released his hand and started for the door.

After Rachel left, Stryker picked up the *Examiner* and tossed it back on the bed. He stuck the Peacemaker in his belt and opened the door. Down the hall he heard Kahla greet Rachel before their door closed and he stepped out into the passageway to make his way topside.

Used to the dirt on solid earth, Stryker had to plant each boot firmly on the ship's deck, which gently rose and fell beneath him. He steadied himself holding the port-side railing, walked toward the bow, and then leaned against it to anchor his forearms on the teak rail. Below, he could see white tips of the waves racing away from the ship as its bow sliced through a black sea. Off in the distance along the shoreline, an occasional light flickered. In the clear sky above him, a massive army of stars positioned themselves in countless formations. Random thoughts slipped into Stryker's head like lights on the distant shore and drifted away.

Rachel's asking him to kill her uncle struck him as, to say the least, unusual. She did offer more pay to ship him out rather than putting a bullet in him. Still, she was willing to have a relative killed. He thought her decision a quick one by a naïve woman. He himself had no hesitation, would've gotten rid of Renard for nothing, as he'd already considered. "Have more trouble shooting a good horse than an asshole," he said out loud. If Rachel were to actually watch the shooting, she would most likely beg him not to do it. However, she'd distanced herself, not unlike the politician who sent a soldier to battle. Sure, he'd kill him if it came to that, but he'd most likely throw Renard on a train . . . and refuse Rachel's payment.

As Stryker mulled over the Renard problem, he knew the motive behind his deal with Rachel had nothing to do with her. It was the same reason he killed Ekard's man, Bill. Money played a part, no doubt, though that now seemed to be less important. He was doing it for Hihn.

Stryker had no friends. Traveled alone, as long as he could remember, never had a use for them. What companions he'd had, besides his wife, and now Morgan, were women, and then only as long as it took to fuck them. Hihn was no friend either. However, the man overcame high odds to get his machine to Felton and paid a ridiculous sum to protect it. Driven by profit, sure, but Hihn's efforts also promised economic advancement and yes, improved working conditions. More than all else though, Hihn sought achievement through his own intellect and effort. He never asked for anything free, he and Stryker had that much in common.

Stryker spit angrily into the waves below. Here, he thought, is a man fighting alone for something useful–and they're trying to kill him for it.

He pushed away from the rail. Rachel's request had surprised and made him uneasy. Leaving her out of matters simplified things for him. His course satisfactorily set, he walked directly back to the cramped cabin, pulled off his boots, read the *Examiner* for ten minutes, and slept 'til the steamship's horn blew the next morning.

The ship reduced speed, the cadence of the steamer's engine cut to a low rumbling drone. Waves, barely foaming, rolled smoothly away from the bow as it angled toward a fog bank blanketing the crescent shoreline of Estero Bay. Towering above and behind the coastal haze, lay emerald green hills dotted with black cattle which at that distance looked like black ants. Farther down the coast, the hulking volcanic plug of Morro Rock, rising nearly six hundred feet from the sea, stood guard at the bay's southern edge.

Stryker stood by the same rail as the previous night with his leather carry bag and a mug of hot coffee, when Kahla joined him with her own cup of the steaming brew. She held it with both hands, warming them. Neither spoke at first. The two of them sipped from their mugs as they approached a wooden pier pushing out from the fog. The pier crawled a thousand feet out into the bay it bisected and lay dead ahead of the steamer's bow. On it two men moved about like ghostly apparitions in the heavy mist. They opened the pier's safety gate and pushed crates out of the way to clear a walkway for loading and unloading passengers.

"Thanks for staying and for coming with us," Kahla said, still looking at the pier in the distance.

"Should be in Felton." Stryker grunted.

"You should be with us." She faced Stryker. "With me."

Her eyebrows arched expectantly, her lips drifted apart; Kahla looked up at the tall man in anticipation of an embrace or a kiss.

"I'm not the man for you, Kahla."

Another blast on the horn drowned her reply. It didn't matter. Both knew there wasn't anything more to say and Kahla didn't repeat herself. She rose on her toes, tugged at his arm, and lightly kissed his cheek. She quickly walked away, her eyes growing moist.

Stryker rested an elbow on the rail and watched Kahla walk to the lower deck hatch. She met a mother and father with two small girls coming up from below and stepped aside to let them pass. The adults offered broad smiles, and he heard them extend cheerful greetings to her. But Kahla's distress was obvious, and their smiles soon vanished. They glanced his way and frowned. However, his fierce features chased away their expressions, and they hurriedly shepherded the children toward the stern.

Stryker looked back at the pier, clearly visible as the fog began to lift. He noticed more crates and men on the platform. The steamer edged closer and a two-handle cart lined with cushions parked by the rail came into view. Buildings on shore began to take shape, stretching southward from the pier, giving him some idea of the coastal town's size. He had no need to revisit the cabin. Except for the horse and saddle, and with the Winchester checked back at the hotel, everything he owned lay in the bag by his boots. When the ship pulled up alongside the pier, he threw down last of the coffee and returned the cup to the galley.

All other passengers, including the little girls and their parents, who struggled mightily against making eye contact with Stryker, disembarked before two sailors came out with Hihn. They carried him with their arms clasped together, forming a chair so that he sat with his arms around their necks, his legs dangling in front. Rachel and Kahla walked behind, trailed by two porters with their trunks. Then, the girls stepped on the ramp without any acknowledgement to or from Stryker.

Standing by the cart, a man wearing a long black frock coat motioned for two more men to help the sailors with Hihn.

Stryker followed them all down and stood off to the side, leaning against the pier with a boot heel hooked on a bottom rail.

Once Hihn was situated comfortably on the cart, he propped himself up on an elbow, and extended his hand to Captain Cass, the man in the frock coat. "Good morning, John."

Captain Cass sported a full head of graying hair and a beard that grew three inches below his craggy face. His powerfully built body, crammed into a six-foot frame, stood proudly erect. The man's large rugged hands looked strong enough to crush a man's skull. When he spoke, words seemed to rumble up from the thick soles of his boots.

"Hans Hihn, ten years? How the hell are you? What you doing on that cart? You got the gout or just turn lazy?" Cass asked, with a broad grin and a hearty grip of Hihn's hand.

"It's been fourteen years, you old *furz* and I am not lazy or sick. Been shot. Tell you more after you get me off this rickety pier." Hihn rolled off his elbow and slumped against the pillow.

The Captain straightened and looked past Hihn. He noticed the two girls, realizing for the first time they were with his German friend. "Ay, and who are these two morning glories you 'av wit' ya?" Cass slipped past the cart with two lively steps. He smothered Rachel's hand which she had politely offered, palm down, in the two of his and then, with a faint bow, he swept the captain's cap from his thick stormy hair. "Captain Jonathon Cass, Miss."

"They're my nieces," Hihn bellowed without turning around.

"We're his nieces," Rachel said at exactly the same time.

"Nieces," Kahla echoed with a laugh.

"I'm Rachel." Rachel laid her palm on her chest, and then she brushed her hand towards Kahla. "My sister, Kahla."

"Tell me, Rachel. Is *furz* a bad word?" Cass asked with a devilish grin.

"Well, uh . . ." Rachel stuttered.

"Means fart," Kahla said, much louder than necessary.

The Captain put his hands on his hips and leaned backward, roaring with laughter. "Hans, ya damn German!" Cass kept his eyes on the girls. "Speak English when ya call my name!" He thrust out his elbows for the girls and, after each niece locked arms with his, Cass loudly ordered, "Men, roll mister Hihn to the house."

They had taken but a few steps when Cass leaned towards Rachel and quietly asked, "That unfriendly looking fellow behind, is he with Hihn?"

"He's Stryker. Our uncle hired security. He can be difficult," Rachel whispered.

The Captain glanced at the tall man with the long black hair, studied him for the briefest of moments, and answered the girls' questions with short responses until they stepped off the pier.

CHAPTER EIGHTEEN

Hank Ledbetter ran a forefinger across his throat, signaling the steam donkey operator to shut it down for the day. He wanted to leave an hour of daylight for maintenance of the engine, pulleys, and cables. When the clanking and hissing abruptly stopped, the sudden silence pounded his ears. It took several minutes before the natural forest sounds sifted in. Below on the rails, he saw night guards armed with shotguns jump off the flatcar and start the uphill hike to the donkey. Six of them. They lined up in single file and began snaking up alongside the skid road. They held their guns with barrels pointed towards the ground. Hank waited for them on top, taking quick glances through the sparse trees on either side of the road, and then he and the work crew headed down to the tracks.

There had been no trouble since Hihn got on the train to Santa Cruz, and that was a week ago. He figured that may have been partially due to Bill's death. Rumor had it there had been foul play, and Juanita had mysteriously disappeared. Regardless, she wasn't around to dispel talk which suggested Bill may have been murdered. Hank suspected the rumors to be more than gossip.

He hopped aboard the flatcar and sat on the edge, his legs dangling over the side. Other log men from farther up the valley had already climbed on; most of them sitting like Hank along the car's edge. A few newer and younger ones, unused to the killer work days, lay on their backs away from the edges, exhausted and too weary to risk falling off. Talk dribbled out in short, labored grunts. Even from hardened old-timers, words at day's end had to low crawl out of their mouths. These men, Hank thought, might not object to a machine which could do some of the back-breaking work for them.

Up ahead, Hank heard the car couplings clanking, one by one. Then his own flatcar jolted forward, as the Shay locomotive began pulling the day's last load of logs and men down to Felton. He shifted his seat and gazed up at the hills, mostly bare except for tree stumps. Some of the stumps were as high as twenty feet and twenty feet wide at the cut. They were all that remained of a mighty stand of trees, some stretching four-hundred feet to the sky, and alive before Christ put on sandals. A shudder went through him as he stared at the hills, the giant trees gone.

"I'm not sure we should be cutting the big ones," Hank said out loud to no one in particular.

"Wha'cha say?" The logger next to Hank, who looked sixty but was only forty-one, said. He sat watching the rail ties flash by with empty sunken eyes. His bushy beard, nearly white, covered his hollowed cheeks. He sat bent forward, forearms resting on his thighs, with gnarled hands clasped together. The logger tried to spit, but his mouth was too dry.

"The really big trees. We ought to leave 'em."

The logger glanced at Hank, and then at the stumps. "All right by me. Hell to cut."

For the rest of the ride, Hank lay on his back, looking at cloud formations overhead.

Sensing the train had slowed; Hank sat up and saw the engine rounding a curve. Two long blasts from the train whistle signaled their arrival in Felton. As they pulled through town, blasts of steam echoed against each passing building before the train finally came to a stop by the sawmill. Buoyed by the prospect of a cool drink and a hearty meal, most of the men jumped from the flatcar and hurried up the street toward Cooper's. Only a few went directly to the dining shack. Hank followed some distance behind the thirsty loggers to the saloon. The big rip saw was quiet, and the locomotive stopped snorting its steam. Raucous laughter with piano players banging out lively tunes flooded the street with each saloon trying to outdo the other. Hank often wondered how the loggers found the energy to carouse the way they did at the end of a hard day's work. Cooper's was the most popular in town. Two other smaller watering holes catered to men who preferred drinking in less crowded surroundings, and Hank, who didn't like crowds, had tried the smaller ones. However, Cooper's had Claire. She showed up in Felton three months before, and, since then, he quenched his thirst at her saloon. She ran the place as part-time owner and madam. That didn't bother Hank. She often sat with him and they talked like old friends. She'd ask him about his past, his family, about the girls he'd known, what kind of woman he wanted for a wife, and never pushed him to buy her a drink or take a girl upstairs. He thought she liked him.

The bartender started lining beers on the counter when the train whistle blew. The men rushed in a few minutes later and crowded in three deep at the bar. Some had already slapped their empty mugs on the countertop for seconds when Hank pushed through the swinging doors.

Claire sat at her regular table with another man, a stranger. Her rigid posture, a tightly drawn face with half-closed eyes, and a smile worn with obvious effort, signaled those who knew the woman–she did not care for the man at her table.

"Miss Claire? They said that was your name," the man began.

Claire offered no greeting in return. She sat ramrod straight, head slightly turned, and stared at him – her mouth, a thin line in stone.

"I suppose you're Bill's replacement." Claire's instincts told her that.

"Name's Albert." He smiled and nodded. "They said you could tell me about Bill, his death I mean. Some say his passing seemed suspicious."

"Wouldn't know about Bill. I wasn't there."

"The girl, Juanita, didn't say anything before she disappeared?" Albert asked.

"You'll have to talk to her." Claire saw Hank and waved to him.

Hank pushed his way across the floor.

"Hank, sit down." Claire flashed an inviting smile that crinkled her eyes. "This gentleman was just leaving."

"Miss Claire, you haven't . . ." Albert began to protest.

"I said you were just leaving."

"If you hear from the girl or anything else . . ."

"I'll tell the sheriff," Claire cut in. "Sit down, Hank."

"Who's he?" Hank asked, pulling back a chair. He'd stayed on his feet until Albert got up from the table. "He giving you trouble?"

"No, but I should have been nicer to him, I guess."

Claire watched Albert approach the bar where he slapped a logger on the back. He stretched himself higher, rising up on his toes, and shouted, "Drinks on me!" Then Albert signaled the bartender and the other loggers crowded in, throwing what was left in their glasses before shoving them toward the bar. The din around Albert rose as men clamored for mugs to be refilled. The new man was already making friends with the loggers.

"Well Hank, how you doing?" Claire's smile and eye crinkles returned.

Hank shoved the chair closer to Claire and sat with his elbows propped on the table. A puddle of beer soaked his sleeve, and he swiped the table with his hand. "Doggonnit," he chortled.

"He's Bill's replacement, I guess. Got to act friendlier. Need to work him. But, I hate his type. Hate what he stands for."

"Work him? What you mean by that?" Hank asked.

"You need a beer, my friend." Claire waved to Ed and mouthed "beer," nodding at Hank.

⚔

Renard rapped his knuckles on the door of the boarding house where he'd been told Heyman Ekard roomed. It stood back from the other buildings, behind the old burned down schoolhouse, at the south end of Felton. The new, bigger school located east of town had teacher's quarters attached to the main structure and the town councilmen decided to rent out the old teacher's home.

Renard banged the door again with the side of his fist, rattling the door in its latch, letting those inside know that he, Renard, meant business. A man cracked it open. He was a stout, stocky man in his mid-thirties, clean shaven with a broken nose and a puffy face that looked as though it had taken its share of punches. Renard thought he looked like a man who liked to fight. Some men are made that way.

"Ekard?" Renard asked. He hadn't actually met Heyman Ekard and didn't realize there might be more than one in the house. He'd talked with loggers from other outfits who said he was the first man in Felton who really wanted to help log men. But this man hardly looked the helpful type.

"Who's askin'?" The man demanded. He kept the door just wide enough for his body to fill the open space, blocking the view inside.

"Renard, Renard Hihn." He started to regret the visit.

"It's okay, Armon. Come in, Mister Hihn." Renard couldn't see who spoke with the smooth as silk voice. It sounded as if the speaker practiced a long time to master the slickness of a crooked casket monger.

Heyman Ekard sat behind a small wooden desk stacked with newspapers, telegraph communiques, and other important looking documents. A well-tooled leather case lay closed beside him. Smartly dressed in a brown suit and vest with the upturned collar of his white starched shirt supporting a scrawny neck, Ekard in his rectangular glasses looked the part of an academic intellectual. A smirky smile looked pasted on his face, unconnected to anything genuine. He smiled with a closed mouth, not offering a real greeting. The corners of his lips remained hooked to his teeth a little too long.

"Although it is unwise for you to visit me, I nevertheless welcome you. What brings you here, Mister Hihn?" The smile hung there, strained and twitching.

"I made it very clear to your man-no bloodshed. My brother could die from his wound." Renard's voice trailed off when he noticed Ekard's expression remained unchanged. He gathered himself to continue. "I can't help but think you not only okayed the shooting, you ordered it. I agreed to help shut down the machine, and only that, to save logger's jobs."

"Sometimes we must engage in activities which are otherwise distasteful to accomplish noble goals ascribed to the common good." Ekard's words came out coated with a heavy lacquer.

"I don't know about any of that," Renard began. "All I know is I won't help any more. I came here hoping my brother's shooting was a mistake. I can see it wasn't. I'm the one who made the mistake. I won't help shut down the steam donkey. I'm through with this business."

Ekard, still smiling, opened the leather case and pulled out a small caliber pistol. He pointed at Renard's chest and pulled the trigger.

The bullet ricocheted off Renard's sternum and lodged itself in his left lung. His eyes flashed wide. His mouth gapped open, his surprise complete. Renard absorbed the gunshot without it knocking him backward, but he'd felt the bullet drill into his chest. His legs grew suddenly weak, and he sank to his knees. The surprised look faded, and resignation with a sad expression replaced it. His chin dropped lower.

Ekard slid the gun in the case and rose to his feet. He came around the desk and knelt in front of Renard. "You stupid fool. I don't give a shit about the loggers. I don't give a shit about your brother, or his machine. And I sure don't give a shit about you."

The fighter by the wall chuckled.

"Tools. Just tools. I use them, used you, to get what I want."

Renard managed to raise his head, a puzzled expression.

"Control, Renard. The loggers, this town, this whole country someday. So now you can die, knowing you betrayed your brother. You lost your life in vain." Standing, smile gone, Ekard said, "Get rid of him. Throw him down a hole or in the river."

CHAPTER NINETEEN

The Cass House, a large, stately two-story building, sat off Ocean Avenue at pier's end. Its wooden siding and ornate gables were painted deep green, matching the sea's hue on a sunny day. Native flowers smothered an arch trellis over the walkway entrance, and vegetables grew in planter boxes inside a white picket fence bordering the sizeable yard. Captain John Cass proudly informed his guests that the house served as the hub of Cayucos's cultural and social events. Off to the left, a red barn housed horses, tools, and equipment. A large herd of his cattle grazed on hills behind the barn.

Captain Cass welcomed the Hihns to his home by rushing up the front steps and throwing open the door. Mrs. Mary Cass, the Captain's second wife after the first had died, was at the door when it opened. Several years younger than her husband, she could still be described as a handsome woman. Handsome seemed more appropriate than pretty, lovely, or beautiful, because being a big-boned woman with angular features, she wasn't graced with femininity. That is not to say she was unattractive. In fact, many thought Mrs. Cass quite remarkable. Her silver-streaked hair and gray eyes fit a woman who spoke in short, crisp sentences. She politely bowed to Hihn, even though he still lay on the cart by the steps.

When guests came to the Cass home, Mary took command, assuming the house and its grounds to be her province. "John, for God's sakes, bring Mr. Hihn in the house. The bedroom downstairs is all made up and he'll go in there. And I trust the girls will find an upstairs bedroom suitable." She stepped aside, allowing Hihn to be carried past her to the bedroom.

"John, please meet with Mr. Stryker," Hihn said, as he was being carried inside.

In the Cass living room, bold furnishings and wallpaper colors matched the outsized personality of the Captain. All the wood seemed to come from the same mahogany cut, the staircase along the wall to the right, the floor which was largely covered with area rugs from the Middle East, and the arms and legs of numerous chairs, sofas, and settees. Ample seating provided for well-attended social gatherings at the Cass home. A portrait of the Captain in full uniform hung over the stone fireplace at the far end of the room, and one of Mrs. Cass adorned a separate wall between two windows. Both seemed placed there, not to grace the room, but to command it.

A long rug ran past the staircase, through an arched doorway, and into the dining room where a rectangular, mahogany table took up most of the space. The downstairs guest room chosen for Hihn was located off to the side, next to the dining room. A swinging door in back of the dining room led to the kitchen. A well-stocked utility room next to the kitchen had two doors, one from the kitchen, and another as an outside entrance.

Mrs. Cass hesitated before she followed the men carrying Hihn, and then she addressed Rachel and Kahla. "After I've made Mr. Hihn comfortable, I'll join you. Please, come in and sit. I won't be long. Your trunks and bags will be delivered to your room and you can freshen up before lunch." Mrs. Cass glanced briefly at Stryker, who remained standing outside by the steps. She saw that her husband went down to meet him after the others had gone inside. She left him to deal with the rough-looking man no one had introduced.

"Name's Cass, John Cass," the Captain said without offering a handshake. "I understand Mr. Hihn hired you for protection. He in danger?"

"Been shot at twice. Hit once. They mean to kill him," Stryker said.

"Who and why?" Cass scrunched his brow.

"Loggers riled up over Hihn's logging machine, but outside troublemakers got a hand in it."

"Steam donkey?" Cass asked. "I've seen one work. Can sure pull a log."

Stryker nodded.

"And so now the loggers don't like losing jobs to a machine," Cass said.

"Reckon there won't be much trouble down here, but he wants me nearby to earn my pay," Stryker said. He'd seen the barn from the outside. A room in the house would sure be more comfortable.

"We can squeeze a bunk in the utility room. C'mon in." Cass extended a guiding arm toward the house. "If that don't beat all," he said to himself, climbing the steps behind Stryker.

Rachel and Kahla rose from their chairs to meet Mrs. Cass coming into the living room. Her husband and Stryker entered at the same time and Mrs. Cass pulled up short, clicking her heels together, stretching her tall frame even higher. The big welcoming smile aimed at the nieces still hung on her face, but the friendliness faded.

"Mary, this is Mr. Stryker. He'll be accompanying Hans and the girls while they're staying with us. I'll have the boys put a bunk in the back room for him." Cass evidently didn't see a need to alarm her by saying Stryker would be guarding the Hihns.

"Shouldn't Mr. Stryker be in a more comfortable room, John?" Mrs. Cass asked. She looked at Stryker while she spoke, her smile gone.

"Should do dear," Cass said.

Mrs. Cass stepped between Rachel and Kahla and wrapped her arms around their shoulders. "Let me show you to your room."

The girl's upstairs bedroom, painted sea green, had two regular beds, two dressers, a writing table with chair, and kerosene lamps on three walls. Two windows, framed with white lace curtains blowing in the breeze, afforded occupants picturesque views, hills to the north and coastline to the south. A painting of the pier by an artist from San Luis Obispo hung opposite the door, greeted guests upon entering the room.

Mrs. Cass stood behind the girls as they looked around the bedroom. "Once you put your belongings away into the drawers, I'll have the chests and bags stored downstairs." She hesitated a moment. Then asked, "What can you tell me about this Mr. Stryker?"

Hihn took three more weeks to recover enough for short walks. During that time, Stryker often took dinner away from the others and ate at the Cayucos Saloon. He used the saloon visits to inquire about new men in town. There weren't any. That would make his job a lot easier, he reasoned. He also got away from dinner conversations where there was considerable effort to drag him into talking about himself. At night after eating, he delayed going back to the Cass House by walking the pier, though he saw no more women standing on ships.

Cass loaned Stryker a stout black horse which he used for rides up the coast. He usually took a trail overlooking the beach. Waves crashed on rocks below, sending spray that sometimes soared more than forty feet, and often with a strong gust of wind, the salty mist would soak horse and rider. Occasional sloped gaps in the embankment allowed Stryker to ride down on the sandy beach. He took these rides alone, but often he *was* watched by the tall, gray-haired woman, using a spyglass from the widow's walk on the Cass House.

During the evenings after dinner, the men would take cognac by the fireplace, usually lit on cooler nights, and discuss business, politics, and philosophy. Captain Cass would pull out his pipe and go through the ritual of lighting it, filling the bowl loosely with a richly blended Cavendish tobacco, tamping it down to about half full, adding more tobacco, and compressing that down to just below the top. He'd strike a large wooden match against a certain stone in the fireplace, the one he'd used for years, and light the bowl evenly, waving the match back and forth slowly. He'd let it burn out and light it once more the same way. After taking a couple of quick puffs to ensure he had a fine draw, he would settle into his favorite wingback chair, all set for good conversation.

Mrs. Cass didn't mind the Captain's smoking. In fact, the full-bodied vanilla tobacco seemed to swathe the Cass house with a comfortable fragrance. What she didn't care for was the masculinity of the talk. She attempted to fill in when the Captain's cohorts failed to show, but she couldn't, or wouldn't engage in a full evening of coarse dialog. Mrs. Cass would, for example, refer to a politician as "ineffectual" when the men thought "jackass" more appropriate. On those nights when just the two of them talked, the Captain eventually slipped into pensive silence, carrying on a debate inside his head. Mrs. Cass read her book.

A week before Hihn's planned return to Felton, Stryker ate dinner with the two families and later joined Cass and Hihn by the fireplace.

Mrs. Cass had gotten used to casual walks with Rachel and Kahla out onto the pier and back. Taking their time, they strolled to the wharf's end. When the moon shone brightly enough, they watched breakers form white rollers in the murky water below. This day it had rained all afternoon. When it finally stopped, it left a heavy fog hugging the ground. The Hihn sisters begged to walk the pier. They thought it would be exciting.

"The fog's too thick tonight," Mrs. Cass said.

"It'll be fun to walk in the fog. We can hold on to the rail going out and back, if we have to," Kahla argued.

Mrs. Cass relented, "There's rain gear in the closet under the stairs."

"The rain's stopped," Rachel said.

"I think you'll need them." Mrs. Cass smiled, as if to say she knew better.

The Captain overheard the women and warned Mrs. Cass, "Not too long, dear. I don't know if the *Wayfarer* has left in this fog. Don't go to the end." Cass turned to Hihn. "Rowdy bunch aboard that one." He directed a good-humored wink toward the men as he returned the pipe to his mouth.

"We can take of ourselves." Mrs. Cass answered tersely, clearly annoyed at her husband's roguish remark. "C'mon, let's go."

The Captain, having three participants instead of the usual two, started the confab with a robust assertion of opinion. "This Grover Cleveland fellow in the White House refuses to aid farmers, business-men, and ranchers like me! We scratch and claw to stay in business and get no help from the government. Damn it all!"

Hihn straightened in his chair. "I never thought of asking federal government for help. You mean they *vould* give us money?" He glanced at Stryker, then back at Cass.

"Well, maybe not directly." Cass puffed on his pipe and then added, "But they could keep those foreigners from bringing cheap goods and livestock into the country. Cause of that we can't get a good price ourselves. Damn it all!"

"He is anti-union and I like that," Hihn offered. He chose not to rise to the same argumentative level as his host.

"Yes, I'll give him that," Cass replied ruefully. Turning to Stryker, he asked, "What say you, Mr. Stryker?"

Stryker paused, and then said, "Cleveland favors trade. He's good for business here and abroad. Keeping prices down for the majority of Americans is a good thing, not a bad one." He looked straight at Cass. "And you're able to buy supplies for your ranch at better prices than you could without the competition."

Cass and Hihn leaned back in their chairs and cocked eyebrows at each other.

The Captain decided not to challenge. "There's a man a little north of here feels the same way you do Mr. Stryker, name's George Hearst. He's been buying up land all over, says he only wants land adjoining his." Cass chortled, and then added, "He was by here the day before you arrived. Had a mining woman with him, good looking thing. Not his wife." Cass gestured with the pipe. "Hmmm, reckon it's all busi-ness though. That George's gettin' up in years. Devoted man too."

Stryker's eyes narrowed. "Did you get her name?"

"Hmmm, let me think. Uh, Bick . . . Bickford! And I believe . . . first name Morgan. Yes, Morgan Bickford."

Stryker got to his feet, and he started to say something but held it. Instead, he turned and grabbed his coat to walk outside.

"The fog seems to have kept your man Stryker from his evening constitutional. Perhaps he's not as hardy as you say," Mrs. Cass said, strolling behind the sisters.

"Oh, I wouldn't know about that," Kahla answered. "He goes off alone a lot. I don't think the weather makes any difference." Kahla stared into the dense, foreboding brume. "Maybe you should lead."

Mrs. Cass moved up between Rachel and Kahla. "Let's hold hands." She tugged on the girl's sleeves, searching for their hands, found them, and gave each a reassuring squeeze. "I've seen him take long rides by the sea. What do you suppose he thinks about out there?"

"He's been with us for quite a while and we know next to nothing about him," Rachel admitted.

"He had a wife," Kahla offered, trying not to step in a puddle.

"A wife?" Mrs. Cass asked. "Who would want him? His looks are vile." Then, when neither girl agreed, she added, "I suppose some women might find him appealing. We should be near the pier. Feel for the boards."

"You sure spent a lot of time watching that vile man," Kahla said under her breath. Then she announced, "I found it," when her foot bumped a plank. She stepped onto the pier ahead of Rachel and Mrs. Cass. "My goodness, you can't even see the lights from your house," she exclaimed, perhaps realizing the walk not as safe as she first thought.

Mrs. Cass and Rachel stopped to look back in vain for the Cass House only a hundred paces behind them. "I hope we can find it on the way back," Rachel groaned.

"Stay close together," Mrs. Cass cautioned. "Do you want to go back now?"

"No," said Kahla. "Not yet anyway."

"Hold the guardrail and watch for crates," Mrs. Cass warned, reminding the girls of freight boxes they'd seen that morning stacked along the railing.

Kahla ran her palm along the top wooden rail, carefully placing one foot ahead of the other so as to not stub her toes. "It's kind of spooky, but I like it. Listen to the waves. We're still above the sand, but I can tell the waves are just ahead. Hear them? Sometimes the big ones sound like thunder. A little scary to hear when you can't see 'em," she said, chattering through her teeth.

Rachel following along behind Kahla, concentrating on not falling, and didn't comment.

Mrs. Cass smiled to herself.

✕

Stryker, surprised by the thick fog, decided not to head to the saloon. Anyway, he wanted to be alone to think. Morgan's alive. That *was* her on the ship. He'd left the town of Bickford thinking she'd died, that he'd live his life the way he always had since Leigh's death . . . alone, no one fettered to him. Whenever he felt the need, he got a saloon girl or went to a bordello. It depended on his mood or how much he had to drink. In his own personal code, he was faithful to his dead wife. He never got emotional with another woman. Loose women satisfied his carnal urges, and nothing more. That allowed him to keep Leigh inside, where no one else could replace her.

He came to the pier. Walking only a few feet, he stopped and leaned against the guardrail. He didn't want to meet up with Mrs. Cass and the girls just yet.

The Bickford woman is a serious matter. Actually, she wasn't "The Bickford Woman," he thought. She was Morgan. She had solid principles, strong character, and an iron will. They had fought, neither giving quarter. A damn good match. And when he held her, he'd liked it. He liked it a lot.

She had a son who despised him. Problem there. He had no intention of raising another man's seed. Cass said nothing of Lucas, though. Maybe the kid was no longer around. She sure moved . . . "Shit!"

But suddenly a woman's scream came ripping out of the fog. A crashing wave cut it short. A desperate, blood-curdling shriek. It escaped from the fog's belly somewhere out on the pier. He listened for another. The relentless roar of waves crashed and rumbled, and he strained to listen, but he only heard the one scream.

He started walking, feeling his way along the guardrail, trying to hurry, holding his other arm up to shield his face, and cursing himself for hastily leaving the Cass house without a gun. Crates and boxes, the larger ones he could feel before he bumped them. The smaller, hard-to-see objects caused him to trip and slam his boots on the boards. He was going fast now, faster than he should. Farther from shore the fog, though still thick, began to thin, and he started running. Stryker hit the crate on a full run. It caught him hard in the chest. The blow knocked the air out of him and he fell to his hands and knees. Crawling forward, head down, mouth open, he gasped for air. He patted his hands forward on the wood, like a dog's. Then his hand landed on something soft. He looked up to see what it was and saw a woman–Mrs. Cass. She lay motionless, face down on the pier. His hand had landed on her rump. He inhaled sharply, filling his lungs. Coughing, he inched closer, searching for a pulse on her neck, and felt a slippery liquid. He placed the back of his hand by her mouth. She breathed.

His eyes couldn't penetrate the fog, but a few feet away he could hear scuffling sounds. The sound of boot scraping and angry grunts, one male and one female, told of a violent struggle. Stryker had just lifted a knee to jump up when he got a hard jolt against his right shoulder. The sharp tip dug in below the collarbone, causing him to fall back on both knees. He fought the pain and drove his body forward. The point sank deeper, but he remained upright. He grabbed the curved spine with his left hand and jerked the cargo hook down and out of his shoulder. Rotating his body left and then violently right, he drove an elbow into the face behind him. Even through the sleeve of his coat, he felt the scrunch of nose cartilage. He cocked his arm again and delivered another elbow smash as the man's head recoiled forward. Stryker ripped the hook from weakened fingers and lunged to his feet.

He skirted along the left rail. The struggle seemed to come from that side of the pier. A few strides brought him up behind Rachel. She stood with arms spread, gripping the handrail with one hand while frantically clutching Kahla's sleeve with the other. Rachel was fighting with all her strength to pull her sister away from another sailor. He was short, but stout, and he had Kahla slung over his shoulder. The man suddenly pivoted, causing Rachel to lose her grip. Losing her balance, she fell back hard against the rail.

The sailor faced Rachel now, with Kahla hanging perilously close to the rail. "God-Dammit woman! I . . ." But then he saw the looming form of the mixed-breed and stopped.

Stryker brushed by Rachel and swung the cargo hook in a blur. The point went in deep, spiking the trachea. Stryker jerked viciously. The sailor staggered a step toward him and fell to his knees. Rachel sprang forward and grabbed her sister. Stryker jammed a boot against the sailor's head and ripped the hook from his neck. Rachel managed to keep Kahla on her feet as the sailor slumped against the girls, blood gushing from his throat. He wrapped his arms around their legs in a desperate attempt to remain upright.

But the sailor's strength deserted him, and his arms slipped from their legs. Stryker grabbed the man's collar, yanked him onto his back. A hard boot shove sent the choking man to the waves below.

Mrs. Cass could hear the man near her, coughing and spitting. He retched and heaved as if to empty his stomach, then he spat and groaned. He was close, real close, and she felt spray droplets hit her face. She inched her head back slowly and cracked open one eye. Less than a foot away, the sailor struggled to rise. With a loud groan, he brought himself up on his knees. Mrs. Cass clamped her eyes shut.

"What the . . . aaugh . . .," the cargo hook swung from behind, throttled the sailor's curse. It went in under his chin and up through the roof of his mouth. Stryker yanked upward, setting the hook deeper. Mrs. Cass opened her eyes in time to see the sailor's hands fall away from his throat. Stunned and frightened, she watched as Stryker dragged the man to the edge of the pier.

Stryker knelt, pulled the hook from the sailor's throat, and rolled him into the sea. He then glanced at her before disappearing into the fog.

Rachel couldn't support her sister by herself, and they both tumbled to the planks. She crawled up next to Kahla's face. "Kahla, wake up!" Rachel whispered desperately, not wanting to yell, fearing another sailor might hear. Still, she yelped when a strong hand pulled her away from her sister.

Stryker knelt beside Kahla. He maneuvered her onto his left shoulder and grabbed the cargo hook. Leveraging a forearm against the handrail, he rose to his feet.

"C'mon, Rachel."

They came upon Mrs. Cass, still on her knees. She'd gripped the top rail with two hands, trying to draw herself upright. Blood had matted her hair and blackened her collar.

"Mrs. Cass!" Rachel ran and tried to help her up. "What happened?

"

I don't know. He hit me. I fell on one of the crates. I . . . must have hit the edge. I'm bleeding." She gently patted the gash and quickly pulled her hand away. "Where's Kahla?"

"We've got her. Can you walk?" Rachel asked.

Mrs. Cass reached out with her arm, searching for support.

Rachel held the injured woman around the waist. "Steady now." Rachel waited for Stryker to pass. "Walk slowly," she said.

Stryker paced himself, ensuring the two women could stay close behind. He saw the town lights beginning to appear through the fog, glowing softly as though shrouded in cobwebs. He hadn't gone more than twenty paces when Kahla began to squirm. Hanging upside down over Stryker's shoulder, she pushed herself away with one hand, closed the other in a fist, and banged against his back with weak, feeble blows.

"Let me go," she rasped.

Rachel reached forward and placed a gentle hand on her sister's back. She leaned closer. "It's all right, Kahla. We're headed home. Stryker's got you."

Kahla pressed her palms against Stryker's waist and pushed. She looked at Rachel and said, "I don't want him to carry me into the house." Her head fell forward between her arms. Then, with great effort, she pushed up again. "Stryker, I need to walk."

Stryker knelt on one knee and let Kahla's feet find the pier. She clung to him after he straightened, to balance herself. "Okay, I just need to let the blood drain from my head. She gazed up at Stryker. "I guess we're even."

"Let's go," he said.

She grasped at his arm and found his hand. He didn't withdraw it.

"Your wife needs a doctor," Stryker announced, barging in the front door.

Captain Cass jumped to his feet. "Where is she?" He saw her head drenched in blood behind Stryker, and his face went pale. "Mary!" He ran across the carpet. "Ramona! Go get the doctor!"

"No, John, it's foggy. Get one of the men to get him," said Mrs. Cass. "I need to sit but I'll be all right."

Cass gripped her arm above the elbow. "Ramona!" Cass yelled again.

The plump housemaid rushed into the room and screamed, "My God!"

Dropping his voice, "Ramona," Mrs. Cass has been injured. Go for one of the boys to fetch James . . . Doctor Dotson. Tell 'im not to come back without him. Let's put her there." Cass pointed at the Chesterfield sofa. "Will one of you girls get a pan of hot water and clean towels?" His burly hand gently spread the matted hair as he and Rachel led his wife to the sofa.

Kahla hurriedly left the room, and she returned with towels. "I put a pan on the stove." She paused to watch Cass wipe off the blood, and then she dashed off again. She came back a few minutes later holding the pan of hot water.

Cass kneeling by his wife spoke gently. "Hard to see, dear. Hans, will you bring us a light?" "Mary, what happened?" He tenderly dabbed the back of her head, soaking more than one towel in blood.

"It . . . uh." Mrs. Cass started but stopped. "Someone else talk."

Rachel took over. "We were attacked by two men from the ship–I guess they were from the ship. They tried to drag us back to it . . .," She recounted the attempted kidnapping while Cass and Hihn listened with stern expressions.

Ramona returned and repeated "Oh My God" so many times that Cass asked her to please shut up.

The front door banged open, and the hired hand with the Doctor following him rushed into the front room. "I ran into him on the way."

"I was coming to pay a visit, John. You must've gone to church Sunday," Doctor Dotson said. He glanced at the Captain and went directly to Mrs. Cass. "Bring me some of that fine cognac, there," he said, pointing at a bottle of Louis XIII cognac on the tray. He turned to Mrs. Cass, "How'd you hurt your head?"

Stryker picked up the cognac glass he'd used earlier, drank what was left, refilled it, and handed the bottle to Hihn. He carried the glass to his room and closed the door. His wound was more of a gash than a puncture, and he began cleaning it with a white towel dipped cognac.

"You opened a flap of your scalp but it's not too deep," Doctor Dotson said to Mrs. Cass. He leaned back to roll up his sleeves. "It'll take more than a couple of stitches, but you should be all right." He opened the medical bag he'd brought in and laid out an array of instruments beside her. When he'd finished cleaning and stitching the wound, he wrapped her head with a large bandage.

"Ramona," Mrs. Cass said. "Bring me my robe and a clean blouse." She turned to her husband. "John, I want to rest here for a while. I'll go upstairs later."

Ramona returned with the garments and held up the robe, shielding Mrs. Cass while she switched blouses. Then, when Mrs. Cass reclined again, she spread the robe over her.

"Excuse me, Hans." Captain Cass walked away from Hihn and joined the women by the sofa. "I want to hear the rest of what happened on that pier."

Each woman took turns recounting the attacks, although none of them knew the entire sequence of events. However, Mrs. Cass and Rachel did describe how the two sailors died.

Captain Cass rubbed his chin. "Hans," he said, looking at Hihn with a stern expression, "It's a good thing your man came along. Those men would have smuggled your nieces aboard ship, and the whole lot of them would have joined in. And, before they reached the next port, the girls would have been tossed overboard."

Two weeks after the attempted kidnapping, the remains of a badly mangled body washed ashore south of Cayucos. The second sailor's body was never found. The *Wayfarer* sailed before dawn, the same night of the attack on the women. A two-man search party turned up nothing on the missing sailors, and the ship's captain, being behind schedule due to the fog, got under way without them.

CHAPTER TWENTY

An hour before daybreak four days later, Stryker waited at pier's end. The steamer cut its engines as it drifted toward the dock. Deck hands cast heavy ropes near the pier's anchor cleats for dock workers to moor the ship. The Pacific Coast Steamer was the same ship they'd taken to Cayucos, and Hihn booked the identical cabins for the return trip north.

"John, I've enjoyed your hospitality. Your Cayucos has provided much needed rest and comfort, but my time here is finished. Besides, *die* welcome mat looks worn," Hihn said, after a long discussion one evening. "I shall miss you and Mrs. Cass, this little town by *das* sea, and these talks. But we need to leave and work at my lumber business. My steam donkey misses me." Hihn chuckled.

"Hans, you and those charming nieces are welcome to stay as long as you like. And I'm sure there will be many a night when I tell Mary I wish you were still here. Your visit has provided much needed refreshment to a tranquil, but all too often, dull life. The waves, though relaxing, can be monotonous." Cass smiled, crinkling his face, before taking a long draw on his pipe.

Stryker had no use for goodbyes. He'd risen early, tidied his room, and left the house. The sun had yet to drive stars from the sky and he stood off to one side with his carry bag, waiting for the ramp to be lowered. When it came down, he boarded the steamer and made his way to his cabin. He tossed the bag on the bed and headed to the galley for coffee. Except for the burley cook and his young apprentice mopping the floor, the dining area was empty. The cook kept fresh coffee brewed, and he handed Stryker a steaming cup through the pass window. Sections of a week-old newspaper lay on one of the tables and Stryker sat to read. A half hour later, he refilled his cup and went topside.

The big yellow orb peeped above a distant hill behind the Cass house to start a bright clear morning. The sea had yet to awaken, and it lay calmly, gently rocking the rail Stryker leaned against. He surveyed the landscape around Cayucos, admiring it, and then he saw movement at the far end of the pier and recognized the Hihn party. The girls led the way, followed by Hihn and Captain Cass. Two men with baggage lumbered behind them. No, Mrs. Cass. He sipped his coffee and watched them drawing closer. Whether they recognized him or not, they didn't wave. Immediately below, at pier's end, the girls took turns politely embracing the captain. Cass then turned and clasped his hands around Hihn's, evidently thinking he needed both of his huge hands to make the salutation sincere. He rattled Hihn's arm for a full minute.

Rachel and Kahla left the men to their goodbyes and walked up the gangplank, exchanging quick glances with Stryker. They knew better than to expect a greeting. When Hihn finally rescued his hand from the captain, he turned and spoke to the baggage carriers, who picked up the bags and followed him to the gangplank.

Captain Cass watched his friend board the ship before shifting his attention to Stryker. He lifted an arm and gestured something halfway between a wave and a salute. Stryker raised his cup almost impercep- tibly in return. He allowed the cup's momentum to carry on to his mouth as he watched the Captain slowly pivot and begin his walk back up the pier. He followed Cass a few minutes before Stryker squinted his eyes to focus beyond the pier at the picturesque green hills one last time . . . and something caught his eye at the Cass House. For the briefest of moments, a white shadowy figure stood in the widow's walk window. Then it was gone.

Buster took the train down to Santa Cruz to meet the Hihn's and he now sat on a bench watching the approaching steamer. A full moon, providing much of the light, had arrived four hours earlier. Hank sent Buster instead of himself, saying Buster could be more easily spared. The steam donkey kept breaking down, or so it seemed, and only Hank knew how to keep it running. Ledbetter had trained two other men on the donkey, but they always needed Hank to locate problems and fix them. Hank and Buster suspected some men tampered with the machine. A missing bolt, a racket pin pulled, valves closed when they should have been opened. It all happened too often. Hank hadn't sent word of these problems to Hihn; there was nothing he could do from Cayucos. Claire said that meant Hihn's own men had started to turn on him. Well, Buster thought, sitting on the bench, I'd better tell the boss what's been goin' on with the steam donkey. And Renard hadn't been around to help.

The Hihn party walked the entire length of the pier to where Buster waited by the bench. "Evening sir, you're all fixed?"

"Buster, good of you to meet us. I am *back* to good health." Hihn thumped his chest. "I thought Hank would show. Everything well with him? But, we are glad you came," Hihn quickly added.

Buster glanced at Stryker standing behind Hihn and said, "Hank's fine. He just thought it best I come instead of him." The huge man picked up the girl's trunks, securing them under each of his muscular arms. "The last train left for the night, Mister Hihn. So, are you staying at the Douglas house?"

"That's right, first train out tomorrow. Still leaving at eight, Buster?"

"Yes, sir."

"Good," Hihn said, as he started up the hill to the hotel. "Buster, how is the cutting?"

⚔

Next day, the early morning fog burned off by the time they got into Felton and the familiar, high-pitched whine of the mill saws and the pungent smell of rotting wood chips greeted them as they walked to the Cunningham Hotel.

Hank Ledbetter arrived with two armed men and five horses a few minutes after the Hihns had checked into the hotel. The two men waited outside by the door while Ledbetter went in to meet Hihn and Stryker.

"Figured you want to ride out to see the steam donkey first thing, Hans. We're cut farther up the valley, maybe good half mile more. That machine of yours works just like you said it would," Hank said.

"We go. You have a board foot count?" Hihn led the three outside.

"Two and a half million, two and a quarter done shipped to Santa Cruz." Hank told him.

"Hell's Bells!" Hihn roared.

Riding side by side, Hihn and Ledbetter led out of Felton. Stryker and the other two men followed.

The five of them rode north up the San Lorenzo Valley, along the rail tracks. Hills, once shaded by a thick forest, lay bare except for stumps. Even the giant Redwood's twenty-foot stumps provided no cover.

"Hank," Hihn said, looking up at the scarred hillside, "we are leaving *die* big trees, yes?"

"Redwoods still stand on the other side, Hans, at least the big ones," Hank answered. "When we head over the ridge a little ways up the valley, you'll see 'em. We don't clear cut like them done on this side."

They rode through Pacific Mills and continued north, still hugging the river and rail tracks, but Hank swung west before they got to Boulder Creek. There, they took a logging road up to the ridgeline. As the five men neared the crest of the ridge, they heard the steam donkey's rumbling engine and its booming steam blasts.

Hihn cracked a wide grin and spurred his mount forward, topping the ridge at a gallop. "There is my little jenny!" He sprang from the saddle, caught a boot in the stirrup, and hopped on one leg until he managed to free his foot. He skip-shuffled the last few steps to his chugging machine and jumped on a skid next to the donkey puncher. "How is she working?" He yelled.

Stryker dismounted and tied the roan to a short, sturdy pine. He grabbed a cup from his saddlebag and strolled over to the large coffee cylinder on a camp table. After filling his cup with the dipper, he walked out the ridgeline to distance himself from the noisy engine. When he'd gone about two hundred paces, he followed a game trail down the other side of the hill, putting the ridge between him and the donkey. He could still hear loggers shouting instructions and the steam donkey's clattering, but the clamor was less annoying now. In fact, since he'd moved away from it, the distant workings sounded strangely good. He sat on a stump and sipped the coffee. It had grown cold, but worth it to not stand by the noisy machine.

Down to his left, he saw the railroad tracks curving around a hill that bowed out toward the San Lorenzo River. The rails continued to his right and south, disappearing behind another outcropping of the hillside. On the far side, a log flume, no longer in use since the logging train's arrival, coursed along the river. Trees too small to cut and tall knolls directly below him prevented a full view of the tracks.

He caught a flash of movement, something black or dark, a brief shadow that vanished before Stryker saw it clearly, maybe on the road or near it, off to his right. He tried to find it again. Gone, lost it. A gully, fifteen feet deep in places, ran up from the road. Whatever it was, an animal or a person, they could be in the gulch, Stryker reasoned. He downed the rest of the coffee and headed back to the steam donkey.

"Going down to the road, back later," Stryker yelled to Hihn. He pointed downhill, dipping his hand twice. He didn't wait for Hihn's reply. Stryker wasn't all that curious about what he saw. If it were an animal, it would most likely move on, and Hank kept several men with shotguns guarding the steam donkey. *Good*, Stryker thought. Hanging around, waiting on a man, didn't sit well with him. A few long, quick, strides took him to the roan. He untied the reins and led the horse down from the ridge. A little over halfway down the hill, he veered away from the skid road and worked his way through shrub oak and berry bushes to reach the head of the gully. The sides of the gulch had been steepened by years of erosion and deadfall lying crisscrossed with sharp branches hid a dry creek bed at least twenty-five feet deep. He stayed along its edge, continuing to lead the roan on down through a heavy thicket of rhododendron brush. Clouds rolled in and a light rain began to fall. The gentle drizzle dampened Stryker's coat, and the rain beading up on bush leaves soaked his trousers when he brushed against them. The roan, excited and nervous, puffed out through its nostrils with a loud purring sound. Its chest and legs glistened with moisture from the undergrowth. Stryker finally broke out of the thick vegetation and came within three hundred yards of the service road and tracks. He'd dropped low enough for the clearing to give him a good view of the road previously hidden by the sloped outcropping.

There, just around a bend in the road, stood a horse and buggy with a black canvas top. Stryker, moving more slowly now and angling away from the buggy, worked his way down to the road where the bend hid him from the buggy. He tied the roan to a sapling, pulled the Winchester, and chambered a round. Gripping the side of the road, where the soggy mud wouldn't suck at his boots, he crept silently forward. Warily, he gradually rounded the bend until the buggy came into view. It was a four-wheeled type with a driver's seat in front and a bench for two under the canopy. The horse, tied to a shrub oak, acknowledged him with a whinny, but Stryker saw no signs of who may have occupied the buggy.

Stryker crossed the road and waded into brush cover. He searched the road left and right but saw nothing. Seeing anything on the other side of the road proved just as futile due to the thick undergrowth. Even though a buggy couldn't carry a gang up to no good, he decided to avoid the road and follow the creek back to the roan. Several times, he stopped and scanned the road. Still, he saw nothing. Upon reaching the roan, he jammed the carbine back into its scabbard and took the reins. He led his horse across the road and found a gentle grade marked with wagon wheel tracks to the creek. The roan hardly needed coaxing to find water. Letting it drink, Stryker moved away and waited.

Clatter of a wagon coming up the road interrupted his thoughts about the buggy. He crept back to the roan and gently pulled its muzzle from the creek. "Easy now," he whispered. He couldn't see the wagon, but he heard it rolling slowly and steadily toward him. Then it stopped near the buggy. Men's voices mumbled something too low to overhear. The wagon started up again.

Stryker took the reins and ran a hand down the roan's neck. "C'mon." He led the animal up along the creek and took cover under bushes growing over a high bank. After throwing the reins around one of the bushes, Stryker pulled the carbine again. He crouched along the bank's edge, using the heavy brush for cover, and waited. The buckboard came into view, a hundred yards away. Two men, one driving the wagon, the other armed with a shotgun, sat up front. Others sat in the open bed behind them. He raised the Winchester and sighted in on the man with the shotgun. As the wagon drew nearer, only fifty paces or so away, he flattened himself against the ground. Better to let the wagon, which carried at least six more men on benches in the bed, pass by. But the roan heard the wagon and horses too. It pricked its ears, raised its head . . . and whinnied.

"Whoa there," the driver sharply grunted. The bearded logger with a plaid shirt and broad suspenders leaned back, pulling hard on the reins. The wagon came to a stop; the lead horses snorted and rattled their collars.

"Why'd you stop, Rolin?" The shotgun-toter asked.

Stryker had seen him in Felton,

"Them horses. Somethin's down there. See 'em? Look at them ears, and the way they're a pointin'."

"We don't abide by no bushwhackers, so if'n you ain't no bushwhacker, you just as soon show yourself. We got eight guns here. Can make a load o' trouble for ya." The driver loudly yelled the threat as he retrieved his shotgun from under the seat. The six men in back jumped to their feet and crowded to the creek side of the wagon. They stood shoulder to shoulder, shotguns and carbines at the ready.

"Shit." Stryker stood but stayed behind the bushes, holding the carbine in both hands and pointing it away from the wagon. He noticed that the clean-shaven fellow next to the driver acted like the only man comfortable holding a gun. The rest were loggers probably, better at wielding axes. Still, the carbine was too slow, and the Peacemaker held six rounds against eight guns. Didn't matter. He'd get one, maybe two shots off before they'd cut him down. Should have run when he had the chance. But he just wasn't cut out to do that.

"Well, well, well. Looky who we have here," the shotgun rider said, sneering. The only man not wearing a knit cap, he wore a well-cut overcoat and a Stetson. "Anyone else hiding in them bushes?" He paused for Stryker's response and didn't get it. "No, huh? Hihn's hired gun out here all by his lonesome. Boys, do you reckon this is a good time to rid ourselves of . . ."

Stryker fired a round into the expensive overcoat and dove in the bushes. The wagon exploded in gunfire. Shotgun pellets blasted holes in his flapping coat before he plunged below the bank. He landed awkwardly on chest and elbows, his chin plowing a furrow in the black mud. Rolling to his side, he pin-wheeled his legs around and came up on all-fours.

Another furious explosion of gunfire followed within a few seconds of the first. Rapid rifle shots and thundering blasts of a twelve-gauge lasted what seemed a full minute. Then the firing stopped. Stryker drew away from the bank and broke into a low, crouching run up the creek. He expected a bullet in his back, but none came. Two hundred yards of stooped running behind the bank brought him to where the stream turned away from the road.

Breathing hard, Stryker searched downstream for loggers coming for him. He briefly held his breath and strained to listen. He dropped and crawled up by the road. No sign of them. He slid back to the stream and propped the carbine upright on its stock near the stream. Cupping water in his hand, he washed mud from the gun barrel and trigger housing. He wiped the mud from his chin with a quick swipe of his shoulder.

Strange, the log men hadn't come after him, Stryker thought. Being curious could get him shot, but he would like to get the roan, if only to kick its ass for almost getting him killed. He crawled back up to the road and lay in the berry bushes for several minutes. After one more look down the creek, he got up and scrambled to the other side. He worked his way up the hill, resting several times behind stumps to scan ahead and listen. Climbing up roughly two hundred yards, he turned south and worked his way down to the edge of the same clearing he'd used earlier. A white pine stump afforded him a suitable firing position, providing both cover and a clear view of the road. Then he saw the wagon.

The two men on the front seat lay crumpled over, motionless. Four more lay in the wagon bed. The last two bodies lay on the ground by the far side of the wagon. Either they had all turned on each other or someone had gunned them down. He doubted they turned on each other.

The buggy was gone.

Stryker skirted the clearing and took his time reaching the road, staying close to stumps and large boulders on his way down. They were all dead. He saw three had black powder burns around bullet holes in their foreheads. Whoever did the killing made sure there were no witnesses. He walked past the bodies of the two men off the wagon. A corner of his mouth twitched. They must have been hard drinkers.

The roan gave him a friendly nicker. "You fucker," Stryker said. "I hope the next man beats the hell outta you."

Stryker led the horse up to the road and swung into the saddle. He took the log-skid road back up over the ridge to the steam donkey, still chugging away with log pulling.

"Find what you were looking for?" Hihn yelled to Stryker as he hopped off a skid.

"No."

When the loggers finished their work day and headed back down the mountain, the wagon and bodies were gone. Hihn and his men didn't learn of the killings until they pulled into Felton. Even if some suspected the mixed-breed, none figured he could take on eight men by himself. Folks around town, especially in the saloons, savored the mystery and chewed on it for days. The local lawman figured a massacre like that one was more than he could handle and telegraphed San Francisco for military personnel to come investigate. He made inquiries, but no arrests.

CHAPTER TWENTY-ONE

Two mornings after the massacre, Stryker pushed through the bat-wing doors of Cooper's saloon. Claire sat at her usual table, writing in a ledger. She had two mugs of coffee on the table, one by the book and one opposite her by a vacant chair. Stryker looked around the barroom, empty except Claire. He strolled over to her table, pulled up the chair by the coffee mug, and sat down.

"Expecting me," he said flatly.

Claire looked up. "Figured two days ought to do it. Also got word you were coming up the street."

"Coffee's still hot," Stryker said, nodding his approval. "Who did the shooting?"

"One of Ekard's men rounded up a few loggers and went looking for trouble. Don't know their names." She returned to her accounting.

Stryker figured Claire knew he wanted to know who shot the loggers, and he also figured she wasn't about to tell him. "Owe 'em. Like to pay my debts."

"Climb the stairs and go down the back steps to leave," Claire said. "Half the town saw you come in here. No need for the other half to see you leave. Some men aren't cutting today. Stay close to Hihn and don't go looking for more trouble. You've got enough coming your way, Stryker."

"Tell me."

"Ekard's got the men organizing a march when the loggers come in tonight. They're gonna parade the caskets of the eight men killed. They plan to stop at Hihn's hotel. Could turn violent. Got soldiers coming, but don't know when they'll get here."

Stryker saluted with the cup as thanks, stood and headed for the stairs. He thought she might throw a parting word at him, but none came. He climbed the steps, walked down the hall to the fire escape door, and cracked it open. The back street looked empty. He opened the door and stepped out onto the stair landing.

There, directly below him, was a black buggy.

Stryker started down the steps, slowly planting a boot on each plank. He'd only gone halfway when the hem of a priest's cassock came into view. He quickened his steps and pivoted around the handrail at the bottom.

Stryker recognized the priest along with the two nuns in the buggy behind him. They were on the train. And he recognized the buggy–the same one he'd seen two days ago.

"You used the shotgun?"

The priest cracked an uneven smile. "And the girls are good with rifles."

"Not that I'm complaining, but saving my hide stirred up a ruckus."

"You know, of course, if they'd gotten to Hihn and that machine, more blood would have been spilt. We just made sure it was theirs."

"Claire's agents?"

"Not exactly. We're on a separate contract with Washington. Better that way. We work together though."

"You're no priest."

"No, we're not of the cloth. But we find the clothes useful."

"And you always dress like that."

"Yes, I've gotten in the habit . . . habits on occasion." The *priest* smiled again, broader.

"You know about tonight," Stryker said.

"Yes, that's why we're here to talk with Claire."

Stryker tipped his hat. "Good shootin'. Keep it up."

"Well, I'm not one to brag . . ." the *priest* said, winking.

"Talking to them." Stryker looked directly at the *nuns*. The pale eyes offered nothing friendly.

Stryker stepped around the buggy and passed two alleys before taking one on his way to the Cunningham Hotel. He didn't expect there would be many folks on the back street, but he found Baldwin Street deserted as well. Eerily quiet, that's how it felt. Even the sawmill at the end of town had the morning off. He figured word must have spread about trouble brewing.

<hr>

"Get your nieces out of the hotel," Stryker told Hihn, who was seated with Hank in the dining room. "Ekard's bringing a mob tonight." He pulled out a chair and sat, picked up a cup, and poured coffee from the porcelain pot on the table.

"A mob?" Hihn exchanged glances with Hank.

"Get 'em up to Cooper's. Tell that woman, Claire, I said keep 'em safe."

"I've got guards, Stryker. Wouldn't they be better here?" Hihn stopped the fork with the clump of potato on it, in front of his mouth.

"Won't be anyone safe here. They storm the hotel. If the shit flies, she'll get them out of town."

"God! You think they'll storm the place?" Hihn asked. He returned the uneaten forkful to the plate.

"Maybe." Stryker answered before rising. "I need a shotgun and shells."

"Get one from the guards in the hallway," Hihn said. "Where you going, Stryker?"

"To find Ekard."

<hr>

Herb and Holland didn't head over to Cooper's by way of Baldwin Street, a more direct route. Young loggers in their late teens, the two lanky, clean shaven boys had just snuck away from the meeting in Ralph Wilson's home. Wilson was there but his new friend, Heyman Ekard, held the meeting and did all the talking. Ekard told them how they would march through town that night carrying torches, shouting slogans like "Vengeance for Loggers" and "Hang Hihn," and firing off their guns. They passed out axes and guns to the twenty-odd men at the meeting. Herb and Holland got guns-weapons they were eager to show Cora and Deeter. Aiming to get an early start on their drinking, they decided on a less conspicuous entrance by going down the back street and climbing the stairs to the rear door. The women said they'd be at the top of the stairs to let them in. The two *soiled doves* had taken a liking to Herb and Holland, promising them a half bottle of the "good" whiskey. The boys jostled each other coming down the back street and then broke into a foot race toward the stairs.

"Stop Holland!" Herb yelled after the quicker Holland. Herb saw Hank's silhouette in the doorway. "Holland! Hold up!" Herb slowed, slipped to his left, and darted into the alley three buildings away from Coopers.

"Ain't foolin' me. You lost!" Holland shouted, then stopped and turned. But when he didn't see Herb, he took a few hesitant steps back. "Herb?"

"Over here!" Herb lowered his voice to a breathy command intended only for Holland.

Holland, only half convinced Herb wasn't using trickery, cautiously approached his friend, waving from the building corner.

"There's a man up there," Herb whispered, grabbing Holland's coat and pulling him in the alley. He shoved Holland behind him and peaked around the corner. "Hey, he's got two girls with him! They're coming down the steps."

Holland crowded behind Herb. "Lemme see. You know who them girls are? They're that German feller's."

"The man with that logging machine?"

"Yeah, it's them," Holland said.

"Here they come. Let's stop 'em!"

"Wait, Herb. What for? Herb, wait!"

But Herb jumped from the alley, gun drawn. He first pointed it at Ledbetter and then talking tough, he started waving it back and forth. "Them's Hihn girls, ain't they? He sneered. "How 'bout we borrow 'em for a while. Our boss wants a little talk wit 'em."

Holland stepped out too, fumbling awkwardly with the gun stuck in his waist pants. He picked up on Herb's plan fast. No doubt Ekard would be mighty grateful for bringing him Hihn's girls. "Your daddy'll git ya back if he wants ya bad enough." Holland finally ripped the front gun sight from whatever the hell it was caught on and pointed the gun.

Hank, who had been holding the pistol at his side, leveled it at Herb's belly and fired.

Herb jumped back, as though he'd somehow dodged the bullet that had already punched him in the gut. Bending at the waist, he grimaced through clenched teeth. "God." He clutched his stomach as blood oozed between his fingers. He looked up at Hank. "Whad' ja do that for?"

Holland froze at first, staring at the growing red splotch under Herb's hand. Then he turned his gun on Hank, firing wildly. Hank dropped his gun when the first bullet blew off his thumb on its way to his ribs. Another bullet found his side, and he went down. He was on his knees when the third round bored in under his collarbone.

"No!" Kahla screamed. She swooped down beside Hank, lifted his gun off the ground in two hands, and pointed it at Holland.

"Miss, don't do that!" Holland yelled.

But Kahla cocked the revolver, and both she and Holland fired at the same time.

Holland took the bullet in the stomach and dropped to the ground on his butt next to Herb.

Holland's round entered Kahla's body beneath her left breast. She fell over backward with her legs curled underneath.

"Kahla!" Rachel rushed to her sister. She tried to raise her, but Kahla's legs remained wedged and Rachel struggled in vain. "Kahla, Kahla." Rachel moaned.

A firm but gentle hand on Rachel's shoulder pulled her away. She twisted around to see Hank using his good hand to straighten Kahla's legs. Then he knelt lower, placing one arm under Kahla's back and his bloodied hand under her legs. Still on his knees, he lifted the girl to his chest, and slumped forward with a groan.

"Hank," Rachel pleaded. She placed her hands under Hank's shoulders and pulled with all her strength. Hank gathered himself and managed to stand. He started walking, heading in a jagged line toward the back of Cooper's saloon twenty feet away. Rachel swept up the travel bags and grasped Hank's arm, trying to help the struggling man stay on his feet.

Hank reached Cooper's back steps but fell forward and collapsed on the stoop.

"Help! Help!" Rachel's cry for help echoed off Cooper's back wall. She grabbed Kahla's arms and tried to pull her from under Hank. "Please somebody, help me!"

The door to Cooper's kitchen swung open. Cletus, holding a mop, and another man wearing a dirty cook apron, came out.

"My sister, she's been shot! Get a doctor!" Rachel yelled excitedly.

"Let's get her inside first," one of them said.

The two men rolled Hank off Kahla. "Hell, he's shot too!" the cook exclaimed.

"Who shot 'em?" The cook asked, scooting back to Kahla.

"Hurry, dammit!" Rachel demanded.

"The cook looked up at Rachel. "Ma'am, I'm sorry. Your sister's dead. They're both dead," he said, nodding at Hank's body.

"No, she can't be. Kahla!" Rachel shook her sister's arm. "Kahla! Kahla!" But the cook was right. Rachel leaned down and cradled her sister's face next to her own. "Kahla," she sobbed. Several minutes passed before Rachel straightened. She rested her palm against her dead sister's face.

"Ma'am, let's bring 'em inside," the usually gruff cook offered, his voice rending the words gently.

Out on the back street, the two would-be kidnappers weren't faring any better.

"Holland, you shot too?" Herb remained sitting with his legs splayed out in front, holding his stomach.

"In the gut. Shit, it hurts." Holland sat bent over his crossed legs in pain.

"Ain't this something," Herb said, his grin chased away by a stab of pain.

"I shot the girl too." Holland lifted his face to the sky and shut his eyes.

"The real pretty one?"

"Yeah."

"Damn." Herb slumped forward and then slowly toppled on his side.

Holland stared at his dying friend. "Damn. Damn all around." He uncrossed his legs and tried to push himself up with one arm while holding his belly with the other, but to no avail. So, he just sat and looked up at the sky again. But the weight of his canted head pulled him onto his back. Lying there, he watched a single white cloud in the blue sky slowly change shape and thought how it would still drift on after he died. Then the sky went dark.

Rachel sat on a kitchen chair, looking at Kahla's body on the table. Thinking that if she watched closely enough, and prayed hard enough, Kahla would move, open her eyes, and smile as she always had. They brought Hank's body in, laid it on a bench, and Rachel's hope for a miracle died with the sound of scuffling boots.

"I'll go get the . . .," Cletus looked at Rachel. "The right folks. Doctor too ma'am, if you want."

Rachel faced the old man, thanking him with a faint smile. "The two men who did the shooting are back there in the street, shot." She was unable to say they might still be alive and needed help.

"Be back in a while, Miss. Reckon them other two can wait." Cletus shuffled out the door to the saloon.

The cook covered the bodies with table cloths. He stepped away and asked, "Would you like a drink or something?"

Before Rachel could respond, Cletus appeared in the doorway again. "Claire's got some people out there. Them church folks brung in a feller they're callin' Ekard. They want coffee. You got some made?"

"Didn't ya tell 'em?" The cook asked.

"I started to whisper to Claire. She hushed me up. Said to bring the coffee." Cletus angrily waved his arm.

"For God's sake, go back and tell . . ."

"Hold on. I'll take the coffee out," Rachel said abruptly. She quickly got to her feet. "Where is it?"

It's on the stove there. Cups and tray in that cupboard. The cook pointed at a covered pot on the stove and the cupboard next to it. "I'll help you. Dipper's right . . . ma'am, let me do this. You've got enough . . ."

"I'll do it," Rachel interrupted.

CHAPTER TWENTY-TWO

Claire and Ekard sat at the card table. The "priest and nuns" and Buster remained standing behind Ekard. When Rachel brought the tray and set it on the table, Claire offered a faint frown and squinted as if to ask, "what are you up to?" Rachel merely smiled a warm greeting as she placed two mugs of coffee in front of Claire and Ekard. She also gave coffee to the others before taking a chair for herself at the table. Both Claire and Ekard stared at Rachel, letting their eyes linger a moment before returning their attentions to one another.

"Why am I here, Miss . . .?" Ekard asked, after taking two nervous gulps of coffee. He returned the mug carefully to the table and set his face in a practiced mask of friendliness, complete with the pasted smile. It took considerable effort on his part because the hulking man behind him had come to his front door with the gun toting clergy and beat his body guard to death.

"You know my name and you have a contact with someone who holds political office. Who is he?" Claire demanded.

"I have no idea what you are talking . . ."

Stryker pushed through the bat swings with the Winchester and the room grew suddenly quiet. His boots thudded heavily on the floor as he walked toward them, slowly and deliberately. Half way to the table he levered a round. He came up behind Rachel and she swiveled around to see him.

"Mister Stryker, meet Heyman Ekard," Claire said.

Heyman took another gulp of coffee to mask his reaction to the hardness of the mixed-breed's features. But a shaky hand failed him. He sloshed some coffee out of the cup and the smile slid from his face.

Stryker raised the Winchester.

Heyman shrunk back, crossing his hands before his face. "Senator Wred! There's proof! Letters at the house! Now you have what you want. I'll leave Felton. I'll leave now." He jumped to his feet, but Buster slammed him back in the chair.

"No, Stryker." Rachel pressed the Winchester's barrel to the floor. She rose to her feet, placed her palms on the table, and leaned toward Ekard. "My uncle brought his machine to Felton for two reasons. First, to make money, and of course, to haul goddamn logs." Rachel glared at Ekard. "But you tried to stop him, and people died. You didn't give a shit, did you?" She straightened, walked around the table, and leaned her face inches from Ekard's. "And now, you want to slither away like the snake you are. No doubt, you've done it many times. But, this time, it won't work. You're already dead."

Ekard nervously swiveled in his seat, searching the other faces at the table. He saw only blank stares. His collar felt unusually tight, and he fumbled with the button. "What do you mean? I told you all you wanted." Sweat beaded heavily on his brow. Clawing at the collar, he finally ripped it open. His labored breathing became more noticeable.

"Not feeling well, Mister Ekard?" Rachel mocked.

Confusion spread across Ekard's face. Then his mouth gaped open as he fought for air. His face turned pale and his body shook. It shook a lot. He rolled to the floor on all fours, convulsing. Choking, Ekard made guttural animal sounds before collapsing in the vomit.

She leaned over the dying man, and when his eyes rolled up at her, she spit in his face.

Rachel straightened and turned to Stryker, "Let's go."

"Wha'd you give him?" Stryker asked as they walked out of the saloon.

"Cyanide . . . from the photography shop."

Rachel waited until they got to the street and she grabbed Stryker's arm with both hands. "Kahla's dead." She buried her face in Stryker's sleeve.

"How?"

"Two of his men-boys. They shot her and Hank. Tried to kidnap us."

"The two men?" Stryker lifted Rachel's chin off his arm.

"Shot. Dead too, probably."

"Not a good day for Hihn," Stryker said, scouting the street.

"She was his favorite. I know." Rachel wiped her eyes with the back of her hand.

"They found Renard's body in the river."

They walked passed Kennedy's Undertaking and Livery on the way to the hotel, a grim reminder of Kahla's death. The undertaker, dressed all in black, and a younger man in a plaid shirt and overalls, loaded the last of four pine boxes on a flatbed wagon.

"She's in the saloon, the kitchen. I should go be with her." Rachel stopped and stared at the pine boxes.

"Your sister isn't in the kitchen, Rachel." Stryker recalled why he didn't go to his wife's funeral and never went to her grave. "When life's gone, there's nothing left."

Rachel looked up at Stryker. "She told me how she felt about you. You must have known."

"Kahla wasn't supposed to die," Stryker replied.

"If we'd stayed in the hotel, she'd be alive." Rachel's voice hardened. She watched the undertaker slap the reins on the horse. She looked down at the ground and closed her eyes. "And, you should have been with us instead of Hank."

"Yeah." Stryker agreed.

Rachel asked to be alone when she told Hihn his niece had been killed. Stryker sat in the hotel dining room waiting by a window, watching the street. Kahla's death will leave a hole in 'em. Tough to see a girl so full of life-gone. Death is so final. Rachel was right about what she'd said. Her sister's killing gave him a shitload of guilt. Damn. Yeah, he'd keep it at bay, but he'd sure feel better if he could put a bullet in it.

He'd finished his second cup of coffee when Hihn came down the stairs. The German spotted Stryker by the window and joined him. "Coffee, black," Hihn told the waitress, and he sat staring at the table until the steaming mug was placed in front of him.

"Stryker, we are leaving. Buster will go with us to Santa Cruz. Kahla hated this damn town, and now I do too. She loved *das* sea and it *vill* be her final resting place." He took a drink of the coffee, paused a moment and took another. "But there is one more thing I must do, and I need you and all *die* men as guards. I am taking Rachel with me to *der* steam donkey, then we *vill* return for *der* train to Santa Cruz."

Hihn and Rachel, Buster and Stryker rode north with fifteen armed men to where the log skid road cut away from the rails and up over the west ridge. On the other side of the ridgeline, the steam donkey sat quietly waiting for the workday to finally start. Hihn, riding next to Rachel, hardly spoke to her or anyone else, only responding in short one-word replies or tight-lipped grunts. He locked his eyes on the road ahead and kept his thoughts buried under his Bavarian hat.

Upon cresting the ridge, Hihn said, "Stryker, get *die* men off *der* ridge–all of them, including guards down by *der* donkey."

Stryker whistled to the guards by the steam donkey, six in all, and motioned for them to join the other armed men along the ridgeline. While the guards gathered their gear and walked the horses up, Hihn dismounted and grabbed the leather satchel hanging on the saddle horn. He shuffled downhill to a stump where he sat, staring at his machine.

After several minutes had passed, Stryker swung off the roan and went down to Hihn. He rested a hand on the German's shoulder. "Let's go, Hans."

"I *vill* be up in a few minutes. Tell *die* others to start back." Hihn rose and nodded uphill toward the guards. "Only be a few minutes."

He went down to the donkey, climbed up on it, and knelt beside the gears.

"What's he doing?" Rachel asked Stryker after he'd walked back up the hill.

"You men start back," Stryker ordered. "Wait at the tracks."

Buster and the guards wheeled their horses and started down the skid road in a single file.

Stryker mounted and watched Hihn on the steam donkey as he spoke. "A man is not finished when he's beaten. He's finished when he quits. Your uncle is about to quit." He leaned over and took the reins of Hihn's horse.

Hihn walked briskly up the hill to Stryker and Rachel, his face grim. He didn't speak. Taking the reins from Stryker, he mounted and started off. Stryker and Rachel followed.

They'd gone two hundred yards down the hill when the thunderous explosion rattled the trees. Stryker quickly settled the roan before moving alongside Rachel's skittish horse and grabbed its halter.

"What was that?" Rachel asked. She looked back uphill and then at Hihn.

Hihn drew a long, labored breath. "They didn't deserve it."

"He blew it up," Rachel said, responding to questioning looks by the guards. No one asked Hihn why. For the rest of the ride back to Felton, each person kept his own counsel.

By the time they arrived back in town, the sun hung above the western mountains and the Santa Cruz train had pulled into Felton's depot, giving the Hihns a little over an hour to load their possessions and board. A horse-drawn wagon holding a pine box stood parked by the loading platform.

"Buster, please help Rachel with her baggage while I pay *die* men. I have a packed bag in my room. Bring it too. We should all be back here in one hour." Hihn saw Stryker standing on the far end of the platform and went over to him. "Stryker, you coming to Santa Cruz?"

"I'll head north. San Francisco."

"This is the last train for a while."

Stryker shook his head.

"Come with me to *das* hotel. I *vill* pay you but I want you with us 'til we leave on *der* train." Hihn turned to the guards waiting by the depot and shouted, "Five men come with me. All the men meet me at Cunningham Hotel in twenty minutes with *die* whole crew. It *vill* be the last pay. Come, Stryker.

"With Ekard and his men dead and us leaving, I don't think we *vill* have more trouble, now that my jenny is dead too. But *vill* not chance it. I want you to see us safe on that train," Hihn said to Stryker as they walked in front of the five guards.

A half hour later, the loggers lined up in front of the hotel, climbing the steps one by one to receive their wages from Hihn, who sat at a card table by the glass doors. When the last man walked down the steps, Hihn and Stryker headed back to the train.

Buster and Rachel stood next to a coach car, waiting. Claire with the *priest* and *nuns* stood by the steps, ready to board.

Stryker noted the wagon and coffin were no longer by the platform.

"So, you're going with us, Mister Stryker?" Claire asked, as he got closer.

"No."

"Pity." Claire turned and climbed the two steps to board. The *priest* and *nuns* followed.

"With Buster going with us to Santa Cruz, and them," Hihn said, nodding toward the coach, "I suppose we won't need you." Without offering to shake hands, he took his niece's elbow and guided her aboard. Neither spoke nor looked back.

Stryker walked toward the Cunningham Hotel and was almost at the steps when he heard the train whistle, followed by hollow steam puffs echoing in the distance. He turned to watch the train leave, but saw only the last two cars disappear around a bare hill. Still, he remained standing in place, reflecting for a moment. "No train big enough to haul my load of regrets." He drew a long, deep breath. "Hell with it."

He came out of the hotel with a haversack slung over his shoulder and headed to the stable. Once again, he took the road north from Felton, planning to cross the Santa Cruz Mountains and drop down to

Saratoga. He'd only ridden four miles in the fading daylight when he saw the logging train. This section of track hugged the road for several hundred feet, accommodating logs to be rolled onto flatcars. Their long work day finished, the loggers sat crowded aboard a flatcar for the short ride to Felton. Two other cars, loaded with logs, trailed behind. The engine slowed, the sound of squealing brakes sliced through the valley. At first, Stryker thought the engineer had seen danger on the track, but that reasoning was quickly proved wrong. Before the train had come to a complete stop, the loggers began leaping from the flatcar and scrambling onto the road. They surrounded Stryker.

"Outnumbered a hundred to one. They don't have a chance." He dug his heels in the roan's flanks, driving it through the mob of loggers armed with axes, saws, and sledgehammers. Two men, one swinging an ax, the other with a hammer, came at him. Stryker shifted in the saddle, firing the Colt, smacking the ax man's forehead with a .44 slug. But the other man swung the hammer, and it struck his chest like a jousting lance, knocking him out of the saddle.

Stryker flipped off the back of the roan and hit the road rolling. He lunged to his feet, blasting the Peacemaker at the circling loggers, the closest men trying to flee the lead, the ones in back pushing forward.

"Let me 'av him!" A thunderous voice with a heavy accent belted out the command. The crowd of men parted, making room for an immense figure with a bushy beard wearing a red flannel undershirt, suspenders supporting leather breeches, and a knit hat too small for the large blond crown.

"Meiggs! Meiggs! Meiggs!" The loggers shouted encouragement with taunts of "Chop 'em and fell 'em! Limb and buck him Meiggs!"

When someone bellowed out, "Pay him back for what he done to Lester and Earl," the log men roared an approving "Yeah!" in unison.

Meiggs wielded the ax as though it was just an extension of his powerful arm. The four-foot handle allowed a lumberjack to reach into the belly of a tree, eight-feet in diameter, and the length of the big Hun's arms added another three feet. When he swung the razor-sharp double-bitted blade, it cut a swath through the air seven feet from his massive frame.

The big 'jack carried the felling tool, one fist below the steel head. Moving slowly toward the mixed-breed in a half crouch, he gripped the handle heel with his right hand and began tapping the ax into his left palm, demonstrating tremendous strength in his knotted forearms.

Stryker was cornered. He'd counted five shots just now . . . six all together, and the Colt was empty. Meiggs surely knew also, by the way he closed in with the confidence of a predator. The circle of loggers grew tighter, but still wide enough for a full swing of the ax. Stryker flipped the smoking Peacemaker to his left hand and threw his right hand behind his back to pull the sai, drawing angry curses from the loggers. Meiggs gripped the ax tighter, no tapping now, and held it at shoulder height, preparing to cut the air and sink the blade.

Stryker felt adrenaline tightening his muscles. He knew if he tried to run, they would overpower and hold him while Meiggs swung the ax.

The pale-eyed killer knew he couldn't stay out where the blade would work alone. He'd have to close with the big logger and fight the ax. He worked his left hand up the Colt's grip, grasping it with his fingers under the trigger guard. He waited for the ax to swing.

Meiggs stepped closer, cocked the ax, and swung. But there was something about the lack of fear in the man he faced that caused him to take less than a full swing. He short-armed its arc.

Stryker dropped his foot back and leaned away from the blade as it sliced by his chest, barely catching the fabric of his shirt. He sprang forward, following the arc of the ax. Locking his arms out straight, he crossed the center prong of the sai with the Colt's barrel. The "V" formed by the barrel and sai caught the ax handle between the big man's hands and the blade, trapping it and stopping a backswing.

Stryker then flipped the sai down his forearm and spun around to plunge the needle-sharp prong into Meiggs' exposed armpit. He jerked the sai viciously, forcing its tip into the spongy tissue of a punctured lung.

Like a wounded bull whose matador's sword has missed the heart and pierced a lung, Meiggs snorted blood from his nostrils, speckling his mustache. Struggling to maintain his strength, he raised the long ax over his head in a desperate attempt to bring the blade down on Stryker before he could leap away. But Stryker didn't step back. Instead, he turned again and drove the sai up between the raised arms of the big man. The center prong entered below the chin and went through the throat to the base of the brain.

Stryker pulled away. Meiggs eyes rolled white, and he crashed to the ground like so many of the trees he'd felled. The circle of loggers stood stunned, staring at the body bleeding on the dirt.

"Stryker! Come with me!"

Captain Talbot rode through the parting crowd of loggers, leading a contingent of heavily armed soldiers.

"There's a man in San Francisco wants to see you!"

ACKNOWLEDGMENTS

Thanks to my hardworking editor, Stacey Smekofske, and to my wife, Pamela Mitchell, for all her unwavering support.

ABOUT WES RAND

Wes Rand was an Artillery Officer in the U.S. Army during the 1960s. He pays alimony. He doesn't like to golf but lives on a golf course. He has been bucked off a horse and two women.

He has a cabin in the mountains where he writes and hikes while his wife plays golf in Las Vegas. Wes enjoys living under the open skies in Nevada and Utah.

f facebook.com/wes.rand.14

instagram.com/rand.wes

Coming Soon From Wild West Books

TROUBLE IN TAHOE

Book 6 in the Evil Stryker Series

LOOK FOR IT IN 2021.

Made in the USA
Middletown, DE
30 April 2022

65029255R00123